Real Life Romance: Duke and Percy

Tara Lynn

Published by: His One, Her Only Publishing

Cover Art by: Dominant Designs

Formatting by: Mr. George Conrad III

Also By Tara

You can find signed paperbacks and eBooks on Tara's website: https://taraconradauthor.com/shop/

<u>Real Life Romance World</u>

Real Life Romance: Gilbert and Elizabeth

https://geni.us/GilbertandElizabeth

Real Life Romance: Duke and Percy https://geni.us/DukeandPercy

Contents

Duke and Percy's story is dedicated to the wonderful booksellers I've worked with over the past
year. Each one of you are wonderful and holds a very special place in my heart.

His One, Her Only Publishing

To: M. Loveless

We at His One, Her Only Publishing are very pleased with the immense success of your books. The demand in the marketplace has nearly tripled over the past thirty days. Emails and letters are pouring in from readers asking where they can meet you in-person. The demand is unlike anything we've seen in the past.

As your publicist, I feel this is an advantageous opportunity for you as an author. A book tour will likely take your already successful career and make it a worldwide phenomenon. I'd like to speak with you about a book tour schedule. Please get in touch with us at your earliest convenience.

Warmest Regards,

Madeliene Bennet

Publicity Executive

Percy

It's a dark and dreary day. I look out the window and watch the big raindrops fall from puffy grey clouds that hang low in the sky while I sip my cup of warm Matcha tea.

Tess rubs her fluffy body against my leg, trying to get my attention. I know exactly what she wants. "We can't go for our walk today." Hemingway, who's sitting next to my feet, flicks the edge of her tail, clearly unhappy with this turn of events. "You girls don't like getting wet, remember?" Hemingway meows at me as if I've offended her before she stands, her tail held high and walks away.

These two fur babies fill my otherwise empty life with so much love. I don't know who needed the other more, them or me. I'll never forget the day the first of the two kitties came into my life.

It was ten years ago, and I was in a bad place. Loneliness and depression were my best friends. It was mid-afternoon, and I was on my way out the front door to grab the mail when I nearly tripped over a kitten. The little furball was curled up on my sidewalk. It meowed and looked up at me with watery-blue eyes. As much as I wanted to bring it right inside, I knew that wasn't the best choice. So, I watched and waited for hours, hoping her mother would return, but she never came. Realizing the tuxedo kitten was an orphan like me, I scooped her up and brought her inside. It was a story of instalove. My little Hemingway brought me something that was missing in my life—joy.

Two years ago, a rescued tiger cat joined our family. Tess, who's named after one of my favorite characters from an Indie romance author, was found with her littermates behind a dumpster behind the diner in town. A good Samaritan brought them to a local shelter. Tess needed emergency veterinary care for a nasty wound on her back leg. The shelter worker told me they believed a larger animal may have attacked her. She was lucky to have survived, but by the time she got medical attention, her leg was too bad to save. The rest of her litter was adopted quickly, but no one wanted a three-legged cat. Except for me. When I saw her picture, there was no question in my mind she was *the one.*

Tess was very timid, so I wasn't sure how things would go when I brought her home. I nestled her in a clothes basket filled with blankets and sat off to the side. It was a watching and waiting game to see how she and Hemingway would get along. I was worried for no reason, though. Hemingway crawled into the basket and immediately assumed the role of surrogate mama. My other worry was how Tess would get around missing a leg, but she never let her uniqueness bother her. The three of us became each other's family.

A crack of thunder sends Tess running and returns my attention out the window.

"It looks like I'm going to have a wet walk to work today," I say aloud on my way to the kitchen to wash my now-empty mug.

Up until last year, I worked solely from home as a writer on Love Words, an online platform where authors upload their stories and readers pay per installment. I'm very lucky that I've been able to make a decent income from it.

I was extremely happy with my life. My cats and I lived a quiet, peaceful existence.

Then everything changed.

The Home Channel ran a nationwide contest. They were searching for a small town that was in need of revitalization. Thousands of towns across the country entered. Washington, Georgia, my hometown, entered and won.

Within a matter of weeks, there was a flurry of activity. Trailers were parked, and tents were erected as contractors, designers, and film crew descended on my little town. Main Street, which had been deserted for years, was suddenly the center of attention. One building at a time was restored, and life was breathed back into Washington. Our Town Square was given a full makeover adding a children's playground, a dog park, a farmer's market, and more. Now revitalized and made popular because of the television show, businesses of all kinds began to fill the store fronts. One of those businesses—Nooks with Books.

Despite my general reclusive nature, my love of books made it impossible to resist applying for a job as a bookseller. I was hired right away. I love my job, but the downside to this situation was leaving my cats all day. Going out to work every day took some getting used to, but book people are good people, so they've made it very easy to adjust. Having an interactive camera hasn't hurt, either.

A recorded meow comes from the clock on my wall—I'm running late as usual.

I race back upstairs to find a pair of shoes, settling on my red-heeled Mary Janes and tossing them into my bag. They'll go perfectly with the black and white polka dot dress I'm wearing. After applying my Victory Red lipstick, I do a final twirl in front of the mirror to make sure my outfit is perfect. Then, I go back downstairs, slide on my pink rain boots, and head out the door with my bag and pink umbrella in hand.

One of the benefits of living in such a small town is being able to walk to work. I even manage to avoid getting splashed by more than one car that drives through the water that's pooling on the sides of the road.

I have just enough time to stop in Muffins and Meows, which is next door to the bookstore. I don't think I'd make it through the day without my usual Triple Berry Vegan Muffin.

"Hey, Percy. How are you today?" Aurora chirps, her bright smile reflecting her genuine curiosity.

"I'm super," Percy responds, her enthusiasm infectious.

"I don't know how you manage to stay so upbeat. Especially in this kind of weather," Aurora muses, a teasing lilt in her voice.

"Trees and flowers need rain as much as sunshine to grow," Percy quips, her words accompanied by a charming grin.

"Okay, Pollyanna," Aurora teases, her eyes dancing with amusement.

Unfazed by her remark, Percy persists, "Is he here?" her tone now tinged with anticipation, adding to the romantic tension.

"He got back early this morning." I follow her into a smaller room off the main part of the café. She and her boyfriend, Chris, converted this area into a feline paradise.

Even if he wasn't perched on top of the kitty tower, it'd still be easy to spot Caspian. I've never come across a cat with coloring as unique as his. His body is covered in long charcoal hair except for his face, which is solid white. Adding to his charm is his one blue and one green eye.

"Hello there, Caspian," I say, scratching behind his ears, eliciting a contented purr from him. "How are you feeling today?"

"The vet said he did terrifically. And he really doesn't seem fazed," comes the reassuring reply.

"I'm glad to hear that. I can't wait for Hemingway and Tess to meet him," I remark, anticipation evident in my voice.

The chimes on the door jingle, and Aurora peeks her head out the doorway to see who's come in.

"It's mister tall, dark, handsome, and quiet," Aurora giggles quietly before returning to the main area of the café.

That's my cue to go.

"I better get to work before I'm late." I grab my muffin and drink from the counter. "Good morning," I mutter as I walk past the man who makes my heart go *pitter-patter*.

Duke

I'm startled from my dream when the obnoxious *ding ding ding* of my alarm clock sounds. Grabbing my trusted wind-up device, I hit the button to stop the offending sound. With a groan, I throw my legs over the side of the bed and prepare to start my day. My first stop is the window, where I squint in preparation to be blinded by the sunshine. But my efforts are for nothing. When I pull open the heavy drapes, I find clouds where there should be a blue sky. And raindrops instead of sun rays.

"Figures this is how the week would start," I grumble. "Leave it to a Monday."

After a hot shower and a cup of coffee, I'm slightly more optimistic about the success of my day. But when I peek my head out the front door and find the rain is only coming down heavier, every ounce of optimism fades.

I sling my messenger bag over my shoulder and grab my umbrella before heading out the front door. But when I press the button to open my umbrella, nothing happens—it's stuck. I press the button again and try to force the mechanism up. Except I force it too hard because when the canopy finally opens, it nearly flips inside out, bending all the delicate metal spreaders.

"Wonderful." I toss the broken umbrella into my garbage can on the way by. "I guess I'll be getting wet today," I say and hurry to the corner so I don't miss my bus.

Washington, Georgia, is a quaint place to live that's full of charm and history. I first saw it while watching one of those home improvement-type channels. The listing said it was a DIY show featuring projects for beginners. I was hoping to learn how to paint a room or build something small like a bar cart. Instead, I got sucked into watching several TV contractor celebrities revamp an entire town. For six weeks, I tuned in faithfully. With each episode, the town and its residents seemed to come alive. By the end, Washington was ready to take on the world, and I was considering taking on Washington.

At first, I thought I'd gone insane. Living alone with my face always glued to my laptop screen must've altered my brain chemistry or something. What does someone like me, who was born and raised in New York City, know about living in a small town?

Nothing, that's exactly what.

Several years prior, my parents retired and decided to move out of the city, relocating to Short Hills, New Jersey. They wanted me to go with them, but why would a then twenty-something-year-old bachelor move to the suburbs.

Fast forward three years, and that same bachelor, who is now thirty, was getting tired of the non-stop rat race and was looking to start over someplace new. When I stumbled upon Washington, it felt like fate.

I really had nothing tying me to the city that doesn't sleep. And luckily for me, my job is remote, so I can live anywhere. Without any further thought or planning, I packed up my things and moved south. I found a one-bedroom, second-floor apartment for a fraction of the amount I was paying for my New York City loft. That was almost a year ago.

After what feels like forever, mainly because I'm getting wet, the bus pulls up in front of me. It's about a fifteen-minute walk into town. But on rainy days, especially ones with no umbrella, I take the bus.

"Good morning, Duke," Harold, the bus driver, greets me as I climb inside.

"Morning," I respond, taking my usual seat behind him. "Not many passengers today."

"The rain usually keeps people inside," Harold remarks.

Except for me. Rain or shine, I still have to work.

The only pitfall I've found in my new home is there's no Wi-Fi. My landlord, Mrs. Custis, who reminds me weekly that she's a direct descendant of Martha Washington, refuses to allow me to have it installed. She does not want wires or a *gaudy silver dish* anywhere on her historic home. It's a small concession to make, so I go into town to use the free Wi-Fi at Nooks with Books. Which I've found is an ideal place to work.

The bus slows to a stop in front of the bookstore.

"Thanks, Harold," I say as I step onto the sidewalk.

"See you later," he replies before closing the doors and pulling away.

Before I settle in for work, I stop at Muffins and Meows to grab breakfast. Aurora, the young lady who owns the place, makes the most scrumptious Triple Berry vegan muffin. I'm not a vegan, but this muffin is too good to pass up.

It also gives me a chance to spend some time with any number of the cats that have a temporary home at the café that also serves as a rescue and adoption center. I'd love to bring one home, but another thing Mrs. Custis doesn't allow is pets. So, I have to get my fill here.

The jingle of the bells tied to the door announces my entrance, and Aurora pops her head out from the cat's playroom. She offers me a bright smile as she heads my way. I'm pleasantly surprised when Percy follows her from the room. She looks adorable today in her polka-dot dress and pink rain boots.

With her head down, Percy grabs her bag and drink and says a quick good morning as she hurries past, not leaving me a chance to return the greeting before she rushes out the door.

"Good morning, Duke. How are you today?" Aurora asks, her voice warm and inviting.

"I'm okay. Would be better if it'd stop raining," I reply, shaking off my wet coat.

"Trees and flowers need the rain as much as sunshine. At least that's what Percy says," Aurora comments with a shrug. "Are you having your regular today?"

"Yes, please," I answer, already looking forward to my usual order.

"Grab a seat. I have a fresh batch about to come out of the oven," Aurora says, motioning towards a nearby table.

I take my usual spot at a table in the corner of the café. It only takes a few seconds before my favorite cat hops onto the seat next to me. She has the most unique coloring—her fur is a deep red. I looked it up and have decided she most likely has some Abyssinian in her.

"Good morning, girl." I reach into my messenger bag and pull out the container of cat treats I carry. "Have you come for your snack?"

She meows in response as though she understands every word I'm saying. Then, she happily devours the offered treat.

"You're going to spoil her," Aurora says with a smile and places my warm muffin and Lychee Bubble Tea on the table.

"I don't mind." I scratch the cat behind her ear, and she purrs happily in response.

Shortly before I left the city, my nineteen-year-old cat, Alfred, passed away. I'd hoped to adopt another one when I moved here, but that's not in the cards. Coming here every day makes it feel like I have a cat—almost. It's bittersweet when I have to leave without taking one with me.

"Pippi's really attached herself to you," Aurora remarks, nodding toward the ginger cat curled up on my lap.

"Pippi?" I inquire, glancing down at the affectionate feline.

"Percy named her Pippi Longstocking because of her red hair," Aurora explains with a grin.

"That's a perfect name for her," I agree, scratching behind Pippi's ears.

"It is," Aurora agrees, her smile widening. "Well, I'll leave you to your breakfast. If you need anything, give a yell."

Pippi hops from the chair to my lap and curls up for a nap while I eat and scroll through the news stories on my phone. It's a slow news day here, as usual. The top story being an article about the new reflective stop sign installed at the end of Main Street. It's a different but very welcome change of pace.

I eat as slowly as possible and drag out drinking my tea, all with the purpose of extending my visit with Pippi, who's asleep on my lap. Aurora has told me on several occasions I'm welcome to stay and use the Wi-Fi in the café. Although I appreciate her kind offer, I decline each time. There's a certain young woman next door that I look forward to seeing every day. One day, I may even get her to talk to me.

As much as I hate waking the cat, I have a project with a rapidly approaching deadline.

"Hey, girl." I pat her back, waking her. "I have to go, but I'll see you later."

After a yawn, the cat jumps to the floor. She rubs her head against my hand before walking away.

"I'll see you after work," I say to Aurora, giving her a small wave as I make my way out.

M. Loveless

To: Madeleine Bennet

I received the email with your request to do a book tour. While I'm equally surprised and excited about my unexpected success, I'm not sure that's an avenue I'd like to pursue.

As you know, I'm not a huge fan of in-person events. I rather prefer keeping my identity a mystery. It's not that I'm in witness protection or anything, but I do enjoy the freedom of walking down the street with the assurance that nobody knows or cares who I am. I'm just a random person going about their daily business.

Perhaps we can meet halfway. If you send me a stack of title pages, I'll sign them in the privacy of my home, and I'll ship them back to you. Voila—you have signed copies, and I maintain my anonymity. It's the best of both worlds.

Let me know when I can expect said package.

Sincerely,

M. Loveless

Percy

MY HEART BEATS FRANTICALLY as I hurry past Duke. I wish I had the courage to look up at him. Maybe even introduce myself to him, but I don't. If I hadn't asked Aurora about the handsome stranger who one day appeared in our town, I wouldn't even know his name. Instead, I focus all my attention on not slipping on the wet floor and falling flat on my face, leaving Aurora to talk to him instead of me.

Aurora and I may be best friends, but we couldn't be any more opposite if we tried. She was the popular head cheerleader who dated the quarterback—actually still does, but now he's an Army Ranger. Me? I was the quiet, quirky girl who sat in the last row and could be found reading a book at lunch. Luckily for me, we were partnered together in kindergarten and have been besties ever since.

Between leaving the house late and spending extra time with Caspian, I'm running later than usual. I eat my muffin in record time, and after brushing the crumbs off my dress, I unlock the door and flip the sign to open.

A few minutes later, Houston, my co-worker, strolls in.

"Morning," he says, his voice warm as he enters the café.

"Good morning," I smile, watching as he comes behind the counter to put his bag away. "I got here a little late and didn't have time to set up for story hour yet." Nooks with Books hosts a children's story hour every Monday, which starts in fifteen minutes.

"Not a problem. I'll do it now," he assures, rolling up his sleeves and getting to work.

It isn't long before toddlers and their caregivers begin streaming in. The little ones rush to the children's section, excited for whatever activity waits for them today. It's almost Thanksgiving, so we'll be reading a story about the holiday and doing a fun turkey craft. So, while Houston gets out the supplies for the craft, the adults get the children settled on their brightly colored mats.

I'm in the middle of ringing out a customer when the door opens. Duke walks into the store with his laptop bag hanging across his chest. Even with his polo shirt, I can see the muscles rippling underneath, hinting at strength beneath his casual attire. He's a unique mix of an Adonis and a brainy computer guy that makes me feel like a thirteen-year-old girl afraid to speak to her crush.

He catches me staring at him, and he smiles at me. Actually smiles. It catches me so off guard I'm frozen in place and lose all track of what I'm doing.

"Ma'am," my customer says and clears her throat. "You forgot my change."

"I'm so sorry," I apologize, immediately reaching into the register drawer to count out the coins while shutting it with my free hand. Despite the distraction, my eyes haven't strayed from Duke as I pass the woman her change.

And then, just like knocking over the first domino, it happens.

I miss her outstretched hand sending coins bouncing everywhere. Scrambling to collect the coins, I squat down but, in the process, bump my cup of tea. Everything moves in slow motion as the plastic lid pops off. The contents slosh about as the cup falls on its side, and the cool liquid spills all over my dress. Things only continue to go downhill when I reach my hand out to grab the counter and miss, hitting the button on the register that opens the drawer instead. The ding sounds a second before the drawer hits me in the head and knocks me flat on my backside.

"I'm fine," I dismiss, waving him off, mortified by the spectacle I just created.

When I get back to my feet, I inspect my dress, which is now wet and sticky.

"Keep the change," the woman insists, grabbing her bag and making a beeline for the door.

"It's not that bad," Houston reassures, his tone comforting as he tries to make me feel better.

"You're right. It's worse than that bad," I admit with a self-deprecating laugh.

"Here," Houston offers, removing the green sweater he's wearing. "You can wear this. I'm okay in my T-shirt."

"You're the best," I express my gratitude, pulling his sweater over my dress.

"Are you sure your head's alright?" he asks, genuine concern evident in his voice.

"I'll be fine. Go back to storytime," I reassure him with a not-so-confident smile.

It's enough reassurance for Houston to return to his not-so-patiently waiting audience.

When I look up, Duke's standing in the middle of the store staring. The corners of his mouth quirk up in a smile before he looks away.

Nice going, Percy. You've managed to make a total fool of yourself.

Duke

EACH DAY, WHEN I open the door to the bookstore, the first thing I do is look for Percy. She has a unique style that has me looking forward to seeing what outfit she's wearing. I spot her behind the counter, waiting on a customer. Today, she's in a black and white polka dot dress. Her vibrant pink hair is hanging in long, wavy curls. And her eyes, they're a deep, dark blue. She looks like a pinup model from the 1950s.

The second the realization hits me that she's watching me as intently as I am her, everything begins to fall apart. Percy's attempting to hand a woman her change, but she misses. The coins spill from her hand and bounce everywhere. As Percy ducks below the counter, presumably to pick up the wayward coins, one of her hands knocks her cup. I watch in horror as the plastic cup teeters on the edge before falling on its side and popping its lid off. The contents empty all over Percy. The situation only gets worse when her hand pops up, seeking the counter. Instead, it lands on the register, triggering the drawer to open. With a clang, the metal drawer hits her on the head and sends her tumbling to the ground.

The horrified customer grabs her purchase and scurries past me in her effort to get out the door.

As much as I want to be the one to help, my legs don't get the message. Before I get the chance to move, Houston swoops in to save the day. He helps Percy to her feet and appears to be consoling her. Percy's cheeks match the color of her hair as she takes in her now-drenched appearance. Then, in a move that would make the hero in any book jealous, Houston removes his sweater and offers it to her.

I feel a pang of jealousy seeing Percy wearing another man's sweater. For one, I want to be *that* guy, but I'm not—never have been. As usual, I watch from the sidelines while the *other* guy gets the girl.

Percy looks up at me once again. That's when I realize I've been standing in the middle of the store staring. I manage to get my lips to cooperate, offering a small smile before I make my way to the tables on the opposite side of the store.

Enough time's been wasted on my pity party. I've been lucky to have met success in several freelancing avenues, including website building for large corporations. My job may not involve going into an office and punching a time clock, but that doesn't make me exempt from deadlines. With that in mind, I settle in and pull my laptop out.

While it's turning on, I pop my earbuds in. When people see them, they automatically assume I'm listening to something when I'm really not. They're a foolproof deterrent, ensuring no one attempts to talk to me.

I've been so engrossed in my work I'm startled when my cell-phone alarm vibrates, letting me know it's noon. I'm pleased with the amount of work I've accomplished. My first project is completed before lunch. I type up a quick email and send the files over to my client. Then, I lock the screen and reach into my satchel, searching for my reusable lunch bag.

Fortunately, the rain has stopped, and the sun is now brightly shining. Leaving my laptop in the store, something I'd never be able to do in New York City, I make my way across the street to the Town Square to enjoy some fresh air and sunshine while I eat lunch.

Washington's Town Square is a literal square, unlike all the *squares* in Manhattan, complete with brick sidewalks meandering through green areas. One side boasts a children's playground, and the other has a farmer's market. In the center is a charming green space with a gazebo and a beautiful three-tiered fountain with picnic tables and benches scattered around it. In the evening, fairy lights that have been strung through the park turn on, making it look like a magical land from a storybook. It reminds me of small-scale Central Park.

I find an empty spot at a table and open my lunch bag. While I eat my peanut butter and jelly sandwich, I also people-watch.

There's a mother pushing one child in a stroller while a second child hops from brick to brick. Several people walk their dogs, while others sit on benches, seeming to be enjoying the afternoon sunshine.

Movement catches my eye. When I look up, I find Aurora walking in my direction. She looks like a woman on a mission.

"Hi, Duke," she says cheerfully, gliding over to my table. "It turned out to be a beautiful day after all."

"It did," I agree, nodding in agreement.

"Do you mind if I join you?" she asks, her movements fluid and graceful.

"Not at all," I reply, though I find her request a bit unexpected. We talk when I go to the café, but we've never been lunch buddies.

She effortlessly throws her legs over the bench and settles across from me. "I wanted to talk about hiring you."

"Hiring me? For what?" I inquire, intrigued by her proposal.

"To build a website for the café. What did you think I was talking about?" she chuckles, her laughter light and infectious.

"Not sure," I admit with a shrug. "I'm kinda surprised you don't have a site already."

"Up to this point, I haven't needed one. But I have an idea I'd like to try. Something that could expand my business beyond Washington," she explains, her words flowing smoothly as she lays out her plans.

Over the next twenty minutes, I listen attentively as Aurora explains her business plan and what she envisions a website might look like.

"So, you want a site that's dual purpose," I confirm, making sure I'm understanding her correctly. "Something that will give the café more exposure and help with the cats?"

"Exactly," she confirms excitedly. "I'm picturing having each of the cat's pictures and a short bio. I'd also like an online application for anyone interested in adopting them."

"That'll be easy enough. Anything else?" I inquire, jotting down some notes as we speak.

"Well, there's one more thing."

"Hit me with it."

"I'm hoping there could be an online store," she says uncertainly. "I've been experimenting with a way to sell my muffins as a mix. Something shelf stable that I can ship to customers anywhere in the U.S. I haven't worked out all the details yet."

"I think you have some really good ideas."

"You do?"

"Yes," I confirm with a reassuring smile. "What kind of timeframe are you looking at?"

"I'm not sure how to ask this, but how much do you charge for something like this?" she finally asks, a hint of hesitance in her voice.

Typically, I get paid a handsome amount to build a website, especially one with the functionality Aurora's looking for. But there's no way I'll charge her that much or anything at all.

Moving here was a spur-of-the-moment, slightly irrational thing to do—something very out of character for me. But I was exhausted from the constant high-energy vibe of New York City. I knew I wanted a change, a slower pace. What I didn't realize was the culture shock I'd have moving to a town where everyone knows your name, and everything is closed by seven p.m. Saying it wasn't an easy adjustment is an understatement.

It was only two weeks, but I was ready to throw in the towel. Until I walked into Muffins and Meows and met Aurora. She recognized I was out of my league. Not that it was hard to see, but I stuck out like a sore thumb.

"Where are you from?" she asked, her curiosity evident in her tone.

"New York City," I replied.

"How did you end up here?" The look on her face was incredulous. "I mean, I love Washington, but I grew up here."

She served me a Triple Berry Vegan muffin, a new recipe she was trying out for her best friend, and a Lychee Berry Tea, and we talked.

"This is a great little place. How long have you been open?" I inquired, my eyes scanning the cozy café.

"Two weeks," she replied, a hint of pride in her voice.

"I understand the Muffins part of your name. What's the Meows part?" I asked, curiosity getting the better of me.

"It's a cat café, or at least it will be once the rescues get here," she explained, her excitement evident as she told me all about the cats that would soon call her café home until they found a forever home. "What kind of work do you do?" she continued, shifting the conversation.

"I'm a freelance worker. I build websites and software programs," I replied, outlining my line of work.

"So, you can work from home then?" she inquired, a hint of interest in her voice.

"I could if I had internet. My landlord won't let me have it installed," I explained, a touch of frustration in my tone.

"Are you the guy who moved into Mrs. Custis' apartment?" she asked, surprising me with her knowledge.

"Yeah. How did you know?" I responded, curious about her source of information.

"Small town. Word travels fast," she replied with a smile, her expression warm and friendly. "I have Wi-Fi here that you're more than welcome to use. But I think the bookstore might be a better place to work."

"Why would the bookstore be better?" I asked, my assumption about her reluctance to have me linger in her café all day becoming apparent.

"My best friend, Percy, is the store manager. And she happens to be single," she explained quickly, a mischievous twinkle in her eye.

I chuckled. "I see."

Up until that moment, I had never believed in love at first sight. I'd always chalked it up to a corny thing for movies and books, but that all changed when I saw Percy. If it wasn't for Aurora, I might not have gone into Nooks with Books, and I would never have met Percy. For that alone, I owe her.

"I'd like to do this for you. As a thank you for helping me get acclimated to Washington," I offer, wanting to express my gratitude.

"That's not fair. This is how you pay your bills, and you can't do that if you don't charge your clients," Aurora protests, concern evident in her voice.

"How soon do you need this done?" I ignore her protests, determined to assist her regardless.

"Duke," she interjects, using my name with a hint of exasperation.

"Aurora," I counter with a grin, enjoying our banter.

"You're impossible," she exclaims, though there's amusement in her tone.

"Okay, how about we agree to a barter?" I suggest, hoping to find a compromise.

Aurora cocks her head to the side. "What are you thinking?"

"There's something I'm going to need your help with. But I'm not ready for it yet. Do we have a deal?" I propose.

Aurora extends her hand to shake on it. "We have a deal."

"Perfect. How soon can you get the info about the cats written?" I inquire, eager to get started.

"I already have it all done," she replies promptly.

"Can you email it to me?" I request.

"Sure. What's your email?" she asks, ready to exchange information.

We exchange email addresses and cell numbers.

"I'll get started building the site while you work on the details for your muffin mixes," I suggest.

"Sounds like a plan," Aurora agrees, glancing over her shoulder. "I have to get back to work."

"So do I," I reply, feeling optimistic about our collaboration.

We walk across the street together, chatting amiably as we go. With a friendly wave, we say our goodbyes, each heading off in a different direction.

Percy

LIKE MOST EVERY OTHER day, Duke goes outside for his lunch break. Normally, he sits alone in the park across the street in the Town Square, but today, I notice Aurora sitting with him. She doesn't stay for just a minute. Instead, she stays for the entire half hour. When he finally returns to the store, he looks like the cat that ate the canary. She has a boyfriend, and I have absolutely no claim to Duke, but I can't help feeling a tad jealous. I'd love nothing more than to be the one having lunch with him.

Enough time wasted on what-ifs.

This morning, we had a rush of customers, which isn't surprising since we're the only Nooks with Books for fifty miles. But they left the store in a bit of disarray. So, I get back to straightening up the BookLuv table. After I'm done there, I have to finish a new display for M. Loveless, the author who's taken the romance world by storm. Currently, they hold three spots on the New York Times best-seller list, and we can't keep their books in stock.

When I finish the display, I go in search of Houston.

"While it's not busy, I'm going back to my office to catch up on some work. Give me a yell if you need a hand," I say, offering my assistance before heading off.

"Will do," Houston replies.

Sometimes, it's tough to manage the day-to-day work in the store along with my responsibilities as a manager, especially with Houston and I being the only two employees. Hopefully, once corporate sees our sales figures, they'll give us the okay to hire more staff. In the meantime, we do the best we can.

Yesterday, the store received several sample magazines. Surprisingly, even with the rise of digital media, we sell a large number of magazines. I'm tasked with perusing them and deciding if there are any periodicals I feel our customers will be interested in. The samples span various subjects, including cooking, gardening, decorating, gaming, and computers.

Most of the decisions are easy. I know what our customers are interested in, and I have enough knowledge of the subjects to pick the highest quality magazines. It's the computer one I'm the most uncertain of. I flip through the pages, but it's like reading a foreign language. None of the industry articles make any sense to me, making it difficult to decide if it's worth carrying.

Wait a minute. I know someone who might be able to help—Duke. It's a brilliant idea.

The only problem with my *brilliant* idea is it requires talking to him. Something more than *hi* or *good morning* as I hurry past him.

After clearing my inbox, I grab the magazine and rehearse what I'm going to say.

"Hi, Duke. I need to make a decision on if we should carry this. But I have no idea what anything inside means."

Nope. That makes me sound too frustrated.

"Hey. We got this sample magazine. Do you want to read it?" I attempt another approach.

Nope, not that either.

I give it another spin. "Can you read this and let me know if it's any good?" I ask, but quickly dismisses the idea as ridiculous.

I flop into my chair and blow out a frustrated breath. Maybe I won't say anything. I'll drop it on the table and keep walking.

"Stop overthinking this, Percy. Just do it."

With the magazine in hand, I walk down the short hall. My heels click on the tiled floor until I make it to the carpeted floor of the store. From the back wall, I'm able to see the lounging area where the tables and chairs are for customers who like to hang around. Duke's exactly where I expect him to be. He's sitting at his usual table, earbuds in, head down, focusing on his laptop screen.

Before I lose what little nerve I have, I make a beeline toward the tables and walk up behind him. He startles when I clear my throat and quickly closes his laptop before taking his earbuds out.

"I have something for you," I say, holding out the magazine.

"Um. Thanks." When he sees the front cover, his face lights up. "This is my favorite magazine. How did you know?"

"It is?" I ask, shocked. What are the chances of that?

"Yeah." Duke opens it and begins leafing through the pages. "When I lived in New York, I bought it all the time. You don't carry it here, so I got a digital subscription, but there's nothing like holding the actual thing. You know what I mean?" He looks up at me.

"I do," I reply. I read my fair share of eBooks, but nothing beats the feeling of holding the real deal.

"Are you going to be carrying it here?" Duke inquires.

"We are," I confirm, especially now that I know it's his favorite.

"This is great," Duke says, his excitement evident as he contin-ues to flip through the pages of the magazine.

Duke goes back to flipping the pages while I stand awkwardly staring, not knowing what to say next. I'm hoping he says something, anything. But he doesn't. He's so enthralled with his new reading material that I'm certain he won't notice I've started to walk away.

"Thanks, Percy," he calls after me.

My stomach fills with butterflies, hearing him say my name. I look over my shoulder and smile. "You're welcome."

Duke and I just had something resembling a conversation. My heart's still beating frantically from excitement when I get to the register.

"Everything good?" Houston asks, glancing over at me.

"Everything's perfect. Why?" I respond, puzzled.

"Your face is flushed," Houston notes.

I bring my hands to my cheeks and feel the warmth.

Houston studies me with a curious look before he says, "My shift is over. Are you going to be okay on your own?"

"I will," I reply, busying myself by straightening the pens on the counter by the register.

"I can stay late if you need," Houston offers.

"I think the rush is over. You're fine to go," I assure him.

He gathers his things and gives a small wave. "Have a good evening."

The remainder of the afternoon is as slow as I predicted. I've run out of things to do hours ago and find myself straightening and re-straightening the displays to pass the time. If I don't, I'll end up staring at Duke. After this morning's debacle, I know that path only leads to embarrassment—my embarrassment.

As I risk a glance in Duke's direction, I catch sight of him tidying up his belongings and commencing his departure toward the door.

Duke

My lunch conversation with Aurora was unexpected. Building a website for Muffins and Meows is going to be much different than the usual strait-laced business sites I typically build. I'm excited to start working on this job. My mind is racing a mile a minute with ideas, but I have to finish the project I'm currently in the middle of first.

I'm so engrossed in my work that I don't hear Percy come up behind me until she clears her throat loudly. I close my laptop, hopefully quick enough that she didn't see what was on my screen.

I'm already thrown off kilter by her unexpected presence, and then she takes it a step further. Then, she speaks—to me. Not only speaks to me but hands me my favorite magazine of all time, *Tek Addikt*. Since I moved to Washington, I've maintained a digital subscription. But there's nothing like holding the glossy pages in my hands.

"Are you going to be carrying it here?" I ask, my voice tinged with hope.

"We are," Percy replies, her tone confident and reassuring.

I can almost hear the orchestra playing the Hallelujah chorus.

"This is great." I flip through the pages and find an article on cutting-edge cybersecurity practices that catches my attention.

Movement from the corner of my eye pulls my focus from the magazine to her. "Thanks, Percy," I say, hoping she's heard me.

Percy stops and turns to face me. Her blue eyes are shimmering. "You're welcome," she says and then continues to walk away.

She's so beautiful. And her smile. It could stop traffic in Times Square.

Somehow, I manage to regain my composure and get back to work until my watch buzzes, alerting me to quitting time. It may seem odd that I keep a regular work schedule with breaks and a quitting time. If I didn't, I'd work day and night without breaks.

Productivity is important. There's no denying that. When I lived in Manhattan, it was essential. If I took breaks or days off, people in the wings were waiting to step in and snatch the jobs I was after. It was exhausting, and I was drained mentally and physically. I worked hard to diversify my income stream—a move that ensures I'll have steady paychecks for the foreseeable future. Going back to long hours and no vacations is not a life I wish to go back to.

After I pack up my things, I start walking to the door. Percy's rearranging a table of books for the third time in the past fifteen minutes.

"Thanks again," I say when I'm next to her.

"You're welcome. I'm glad you like it."

Everything is right in Duke Kennedy's world as I make my second stop at the café to grab another muffin and tea for the bus ride home. While I'm there, I also make sure to stop and give Pippi another treat.

"She really likes you," Aurora says as she packs my muffin. "Maybe I can talk to Mrs. Custis and see if I can get her to change her mind."

"Thanks for the offer. But I've tried everything. I even offered to pay for the apartment to be professionally cleaned when I move out, but she refuses to budge."

"I'm sorry."

"Yeah, me too." I give Pippi a final scratch behind the ear. "I'll see you tomorrow, girl."

His One, Her Only Publishing

To: M. Loveless

I appreciate your willingness to help get signed books into the hands of your fans. Your idea of signing title pages is excellent, and I applaud you for thinking out of the box. Our printer had five thousand title pages printed. They've already been sent out to you. If you would sign them at your earliest convenience and return them to us. For your convenience, there's a postage-paid label in each box. The special editions will be available exclusively through Nooks with Books.

However, I'm still requesting we discuss your making public appearances. Your books are obviously doing phenomenal, as shown by your sales figures, and holding three of the top spots on the New York Times bestseller list. That's quite an accomplishment. This is also why I strongly feel doing a book tour is important.

We at His One, Her Only Publishing understand your request to keep your identity a secret. Something I feel has played a role in your rise in popularity—everyone loves a good mystery. But every mystery must come to an end. Now is the optimal time to reveal your identity and allow your fans to meet their favorite author. I firmly believe this will skyrocket not only your backlist but your upcoming release as well.

I've attached the proposed schedule for your consideration.

Please respond at your earliest convenience with any proposed changes you might have. We want to get this book tour kicked off for the holiday shopping season.

Warmest Regards,

Madeliene Bennet

Publicity Executive

M. Loveless

To: Madeline Bennet

I will keep an eye on my mail for the package. I'm glad you will be offering these special editions solely through Nooks with Books, as I am particularly fond of that company.

I looked at the proposed schedule you sent. Regretfully, I must insist that a book tour is still not something I'm willing to do.

Sincerely,

M. Loveless

Percy

Two. That's the number of conversations Duke and I had today. Listening to his deep voice makes me feel like I have a dozen sparkly butterflies in my belly. And when he looks at me with his hazel eyes, it's all I can do to not swoon. Duke's not only gorgeous but also sweet and smart—he's the whole package wrapped up in one man. I've overheard women in the store whispering to one another about the hot computer geek that's here all the time.

Duke's still sitting on the bench at the bus stop when I leave work. In another life, I'd walk over and talk to him. I'd do what I daydream about and ask him out. Who am I kidding? I barely worked up the nerve to say a few sentences to him about a magazine. How in the world would I get the courage to ask him out?

"Hey Percy," Aurora greets me as I walk into the café.

"Hi," I respond absentmindedly, watching out the window as the bus pulls up. Duke climbs the steps and disappears inside.

"Earth to Percy." Aurora waves her hand in front of my face, breaking my trance.

"What?" I turn my attention back to her.

"Why don't you just talk to him? He's not going to bite," she remarks, nudging me gently.

"I did," I admit.

"You did what?" Aurora's eyes widen with curiosity.

"I talked to him this afternoon," I clarify.

"Shut up. No, don't shut up," Aurora says excitedly. "Sit. I need all the details."

The café is closed for the day, so it's just Aurora and me. "We got some sample magazines in today." I take a seat at an empty table while she grabs us both a drink. "One was a tech magazine. I didn't know if it was worth carrying or not, so I gave it to Duke. Turns out, it's his favorite."

"Well, that's a step in the right direction." She sets our teas on the table and sits across from me. "A baby step, but a step, nonetheless. I think you should go for it. Just ask him out."

"As if." I roll my eyes. "I'd get all tongue-tied and mess it up. Nope. Can't do it." Caspian strolls out of the playroom, interrupting our conversation. "There's my handsome boy." He gingerly jumps on my lap, purring loudly.

"Don't change the subject," Aurora insists, her tone firm.

"Ror, I'm not like you. I can't just go up to a guy and ask him if he'd like to go out. Especially a guy like Duke," I admit, feeling a bit defeated.

"It's really not that hard," Aurora counters, her confidence unwavering.

I realize I'm not going to win this argument with her, so instead, I opt for a subject change. "Have you heard from Chris?"

"He got a very short phone call through yesterday," Aurora responds, her expression softening with affection. "He's doing good. Can't wait to get home."

"When's his deployment over?" I inquire, genuinely interested.

"One month left. And yes, I'm counting the days," Aurora replies with a smile, her anticipation palpable.

Chris and Aurora have been together since high school. They met at the homecoming football game when she was a freshman and Chris was a junior. He was the handsome quarterback, and she was a gorgeous and outgoing cheerleader. It came as no surprise the two hit it off and started dating.

After Chris graduated, he joined the military. The Army, to be exact. He had his sights set on becoming an Army Ranger—which is no small feat. He worked his way through all the special trainings and achieved his goal. Being a Ranger is a serious commitment. He often has long deployments. This one was for a year. An entire year where Aurora doesn't know exactly where he's at or what he's doing. The Rangers are super secretive like that. Even when Chris is home, he isn't able to let the proverbial cat out of the bag and tell her anything. She lives for his phone calls, which are often few and far between. I don't know how Aurora stays so strong. I'd never be able to handle it.

I shift in my seat, and Caspian jumps off my lap. He walks over to the door and begins rubbing himself against it.

"Looks like someone's ready to go." Aurora gets up and goes behind the counter. "I have his going home bag for you."

Aurora takes her job as temporary guardian over all these cats very seriously. In addition to providing them top-notch accommodations while they're residents at Muffins and Meows, she's also struck up a partnership with Dr. Rob, a local vet who's as invested in rescues as she is. He makes sure each cat is healthy, up-to-date on immunizations, and spayed or neutered before they can be adopted. Prospective adoptees are put through a lengthy process to ensure they understand the responsibilities of pet ownership as well as their ability to provide a safe and loving forever home for a kitty. Once a person is approved, they are invited to come in and spend some time with the cats. Aurora wants to ensure a good match, for both the human and the feline, is made. The hope is for every one of the cats to go to its forever home. But even if they continue to reside at the café, they'll never lack for care or love.

While Aurora reviews the vet's instructions for Caspian's after-surgery care, I reach into my bag and pull out the new harness and leash I bought. I'm not a big fan of cat carriers. I prefer to let my furry friends walk with me, exploring everything about them. Passersby are always shocked by how curious my girls are when they're out on a walk. I'm certain once Caspian gets acclimated, he'll enjoy it just as much as the girls.

Slowly, so I don't scare him, I put the harness over his neck and shoulders and make sure it's a snug fit. I don't want him to slip out and run off. Then, I clip the thin leash on and set him on the floor so he can have a few minutes to get used to it. One would have to look closely to figure out if he's a statue or a real cat, but I can see his little brain working. It's trying to process what this new attachment is and what, if anything, he's supposed to do about it.

"Here's his bag." Aurora hands me a reusable fabric bag with tiny cat prints on it. "His vaccination record and microchip info are all in there."

"Thanks for taking such good care of him," I express my gratitude, pulling my friend into a hug.

Aurora squats down and calls Caspian. He moves his eyes, but his body is still frozen in place. I'm beginning to think I'll be carrying him home. But then he stands and walks over to Aurora. Despite his initial uncertainty, he's not fazed by the harness or the leash.

"Look at your Narnia leash. You look so handsome. I'm going to miss you." She kisses the top of his head. "But you're going to a great home. And we're both in luck because she's also my best friend, so we'll get to see each other." Aurora wipes a stray tear.

"Don't cry. You're at my house all the time. You'll see him plenty," I reassure, offering Aurora some comfort.

"I know. But goodbyes are never easy," Aurora replies, her voice tinged with sadness.

"Call it a see ya later, then," I suggest optimistically. I reach down and grab Caspian's leash. "Do you want to come over and help me get him settled in?"

"I wish I could, but I promised my dad I'd go to his house for dinner," Aurora regrets, sounding torn.

"Next time," I promise, understanding Aurora's commitment. I start walking toward the door. "Caspian and I are off on our first adventure. See ya tomorrow."

Percy

CASPIAN DID SURPRISINGLY WELL on our walk home. I don't know much about his history other than someone left him at a shelter. But like so many other shelters, they were already at max capacity. They were going to do the unthinkable until Kitty Whisker Warriors stepped in. They also happen to be one of the rescues Aurora works with. They're responsible for bringing him to the café. And I'm so glad they did because the second I saw him, I knew we were meant to be together.

"Alright, Cas. Ready to meet your older sisters?" I lift him into my arms. "Fingers and paws crossed it goes well."

Then, I unlock the door and step into the house. Like every other day, Hemingway and Tess are waiting to welcome me home. It only takes a second for them to notice the fluffy black bundle in my arms. Said bundle also notices them and lets out a small growl. But my happy-go-lucky girls are unphased by Caspian's lack of enthusiasm. I, too, ignore his complaint and continue walking through the house with Hemingway and Tess on my tail. I sit on the couch with Caspian on my lap for the official meet and greet.

As soon as I remove the harness, Caspian crawls off my lap and stands on the cushion next to me. He's wary of the girls who approach to inspect the stranger. Without warning, Tess jumps onto the couch next to him and begins her sniffing assessment. Caspian gives her the side eye, obviously not amused with forward behavior. It's clear he's passed her test when she rubs up against him, purring.

Hemingway, who is the dominant cat in the house, isn't as easy to convince that my bringing home a little brother was indeed a good idea. She rolls around my feet, trying to divert my attention from the unwelcome intruder. Caspian lays down and peers over the edge of the cushion, watching the goofy girl before he jumps down next to her.

I hold my breath, hoping a fight doesn't break out. I'm shocked watching my bossy girl submit to the new *prince*, earning a nuzzle from him in response. I let out the breath I was holding.

"Are you boys and girls hungry?" I ask my new trio.

My felines demonstrate their above-average intelligence by meowing in response to my question. Caspian follows the girls, who follow me in our little parade to the kitchen cupboard holding the cans of kitty chow. While I'm filling their bowls, my stomach growls, and I realize I skipped lunch today.

"Should I cook or defrost something?" Even though it's only me here, I love cooking. I always make extra for lunches and to freeze for a meal another night. This way, I'm never at a loss for a home-cooked meal. It's another one of those things I've carried with me since childhood.

I learned to cook at a relatively young age. It was something I chose to learn to ease the burden on my dad.

Mom left Dad and me right before my tenth birthday. Like Dad, she grew up in Washington, but she was restless and didn't want to stay in our small town. Dad was happy here. He was the chief of police and earned a good salary. One that allowed them to own a house with a literal white picket fence. And Washington is the ideal town to raise a family. None of that mattered to Mom, though. She had a dream of a life that was bigger and better.

I'll never forget the day.

I walked home from school and expected to find Mom on the porch waiting for me like she did every day. Except that day, she wasn't there. I got that feeling in the pit of my stomach. You know, the one where you just know something isn't right? I stood at the bottom of the four wood steps with their brown paint that was beginning to peel for what felt like forever.

Finally, I found the courage to climb the steps.

With shaking hands, I reached out and grabbed the doorknob. It turned—it was unlocked. Pushing it open, I walked into the house and was met with silence. From the doorway, I could see straight into the kitchen. There was a white envelope propped up against the salt and pepper shakers on the counter.

I didn't touch it—didn't have to. I knew exactly what it said.

My mother was gone.

She left.

She didn't love me enough to stay.

My heart shattered into a million pieces.

The pink backpack with the unicorn charm on the zipper pull slid off my shoulders, landing with a thud on the foyer floor. Taking the steps two at a time, I ran to my room, where I screamed until my voice went hoarse. The dam burst, and I dropped to my knees and cried.

I was still crying when I heard the front door open and close—Dad was home. His heart was about to break just as mine was. Dad was silent for the longest time. I guessed he was reading whatever note Mom left.

The old stairs creaked as he walked up slowly. His footsteps grew louder as he came down the hall to my bedroom. My door opened, and the next thing I knew, Dad was on my floor, holding me while I cried myself to sleep.

I never asked him what the note said. He never offered.

That was the first and last time I shed tears over my mom leaving.

That day changed everything.

Dad and I were forced to find a new normal. Dad assumed the role of both mom and dad, and I had to grow up a little quicker.

Although he never asked me to, I willingly took on the housework my mother would've done. After school, I'd come straight home and do my homework. Instead of going outside to play with my friends, I'd do a load of laundry and make sure the house remained tidied. Most of my friends moved on without me. Except for Aurora. She was the only one who stuck by my side—the only one who understood. Because she didn't have a mom anymore, either.

It was during that time I learned to cook. Dad's job often required him to work overtime. So, rather than waiting for him to get home from work and have him cook, I pulled out the cookbooks and taught myself. We had our fair share of overcooked meals, but Dad never complained. On his days off, he'd join me in the kitchen, teaching me things you can't learn from a book.

Not a day went by without Dad making sure I knew how much he appreciated everything I did.

Sadly, I lost my father right after my eighteenth birthday.

It was a warm spring Sunday afternoon. We were outside doing yard work. Dad was pushing the lawnmower when he dropped to the ground. He suffered a fatal heart attack.

I didn't get the chance to say goodbye.

He was just gone.

I shake my head to dispel the sad memories. I don't like dwelling on the past. No good ever comes from it.

Deciding I'm in the mood to cook, I look through the ingredients in the kitchen. As much as possible, I try to shop the seasons. I have a shiny eggplant that will make a delicious parmesan with a side of vegan pasta. There will be enough for dinner. I'll freeze several portions and bring some to Aurora tomorrow.

Duke

"Good morning, Duke," Harold greets me with a smile.

"Morning," I respond, taking a seat behind him.

"It's a beautiful day. Why do you seem so down?" Harold asks, concern evident in his tone.

"I guess I got out on the wrong side of the bed this morning." It was just one of those mornings that, despite the sunshine, I wasn't feeling it. I almost didn't come into town, but at the last minute, I threw some clothes on and left the house. However, my hair is a bit disheveled, and I didn't shave.

"Well, cheer up, good buddy. The holiday season will be upon us in just a few weeks," Harold says, trying to lift my spirits.

"Oh yeah. I almost forgot," I reply, the reminder bringing a faint smile to my face.

I've never lived in a warm climate, and if we took a holiday trip, we went north, where it was even colder. The days leading up to Thanksgiving were filled with crisp, cool air and colored leaves floating on the breeze. And I can't forget the Macy's Day Parade. Every year, my parents and I braved the crowds to see the parade in person.

As Christmas drew near, the colors of fall disappeared, and in its place were the sights and smells of winter. Snowflakes did a familiar dance as they fell, covering the ground in a layer of white. But here, it's still eighty degrees and sunny, and Thanksgiving's next week. It's a very odd feeling, indeed.

"Do you have plans for Turkey Day?" Harold asks as the bus pulls up to my stop.

"I might take the day off and watch the parade on television," I reply, preparing to disembark.

"You aren't having company? Or a big meal?" Harold inquires, his eyebrows raised with interest.

I was planning on flying to New Jersey to stay with my parents for Thanksgiving. But when I spoke to them yesterday, my mom informed me they were breaking tradition this year. Instead of a big turkey dinner, they booked a Caribbean cruise. I was stunned. Completely speechless. I didn't even know my parents liked cruising.

"Nope," I say as I walk down the steps. "Have a nice day, Harold."

Of course, they offered to change their plans and stay home if I was going to be alone for the holiday. They sounded so excited, and I didn't have the heart to disappoint them. So, I told them I was calling to let them know I wouldn't be coming home and that I was spending the holiday with friends here. They were so relieved. I knew that even though it wasn't the truth, it was the right thing to do. They worked hard for so many years. They deserve to travel and have the time of their lives.

But that does leave me alone.

"Morning, Duke," Aurora chirps when I walk into the café for breakfast.

"Morning," I reply, trying to muster a smile.

"I have your muffin warming for you. Grab a seat and—" She stops what she's doing and takes in my appearance. "What's wrong?"

"Just a rough morning, is all," I admit, feeling a weight on my shoulders.

"I see," Aurora responds sympathetically, her expression softening with concern.

The bells on the door jingle. We both turn and watch as Percy walks in.

Today, she's wearing a shorter dress with three pumpkins on the front. Covering her legs are orange tights that also have pumpkins. She's wearing a pair of shiny black shoes, the same style she wears frequently. I think they're called Mary Lou's or something like that.

"Morning, Percy," Aurora says just as the timer for the warming oven sounds.

"Morning," she replies with a smile.

"You're early today," Aurora observes as she sets my muffin and tea on the table.

"Thank you," I say quietly, feeling grateful for the gesture.

"Duke and I were just sitting down for breakfast. Would you like to join us?" Aurora offers kindly.

"I don't know," I say hesitantly, feeling a bit unsure.

"You have plenty of time. Grab a seat," Aurora encourages, nudging me toward the table where Duke is sitting. "I'll grab you a muffin."

Percy sits across from me and offers a shy smile. Just as I'm about to say something to Percy, Pippi strolls over, stealing her attention.

"Hey, girl," Percy says, reaching down to pet the cat, but she walks straight past her and hops on my lap.

"And I thought you and I were friends," Percy pouts playfully.

Aurora laughs as she sets Percy's breakfast down. "Duke is her most favorite human."

"I see that," Percy says with a mock frown.

"It's only because I bring her treats," I interject, pulling a container from my bag and emptying a treat into my hand. Pippi greedily takes it from me and devours it, then meows for more.

"She adores him. But unfortunately, he's not allowed to have pets," Aurora explains.

"That's awful," Percy sympathizes.

"It's not ideal, but at least I get to visit her here. That is until she gets adopted," I say, trying to sound upbeat, though I can't help feeling a twinge of jealousy at the thought of Pippi leaving.

"Since we're all here," Aurora changes the subject, "let's talk about Friendsgiving. Do you have plans, Duke?"

"Me? I'm going to have a quiet day at home," I reply.

"Alone?" Aurora questions.

"Yes," I confirm, taking a bite of my muffin.

"That won't do at all. Will it, Percy?" Aurora turns to Percy for agreement.

Percy looks at her friend with wide eyes. "Um. No? I mean, no, that won't do."

"That settles it. You'll come to Percy's with my dad and me. Houston and his mom will be there, too. No one should be alone on a holiday," Aurora decides firmly.

I look between the girls, not sure what to say. "I don't want to impose."

"It's no imposition. Is it, Percy?" Aurora asks.

"Not at all. We'd love to have you," Percy assures me, her blue eyes meeting mine and disarming me completely.

"Okay, then. I'd love to come," I agree with a smile.

"Great. My dad and I will pick you up," Aurora announces happily.

And somehow, just like that, I'm going to Percy's house for Friendsgiving. I also make a mental note to do an internet search on what a *Friendsgiving* is.

Percy

I'VE BEEN SO CAUGHT up in the conversation I totally forgot about work. When I finally check the time, I jump from my seat. "I have to run." I grab my uneaten muffin. "I need to get the store open."

"See ya later." Aurora waves.

I'm still in shock as I dig through my bag, searching for the keys to the store. I'm not sure how Aurora managed it, but Duke is coming to my house for Thanksgiving next week.

Oh. My. God.

Duke is coming to *my* house for Thanksgiving.

I feel like a schoolgirl whose crush has just asked her to the Friday night dance. I wish Houston were here. I'm dying to tell someone else about it. I need to be sure it wasn't all in my imagination.

Percy:

Did that really happen?

Aurora:

Did what happen?

Percy:

Did you really invite Duke to my house for Friendsgiving, and he actually said yes?

Aurora:

Yes. Why are you so surprised?

Percy:

I didn't think he'd want to spend a holiday with me.

Aurora:

I told you he likes you.

Percy:

You did. Gotta run. Customers are here.

Although there's no rule about employees and cell phones, I don't like to have mine out when there are customers in the store. So, I slip it into my pocket and get to work.

It turns out to be a fairly busy mid-morning. Dukes at his usual table doing whatever work he does on his laptop all day. Several other customers are sitting at the other tables and chairs, reading books and magazines. One of my favorite things about the environment in the store is that customers aren't expected to make a purchase and leave. We welcome our customers to grab a book and stay a while.

If I had my way, and maybe someday I will. I'd convince the home office to open the wall that connects up to Muffins and Meows so our customers could grab a tea or coffee and a kitty to snuggle with while they're in the store. It would make an already wonderful environment even better.

I didn't think the line at the register would die down, but I've finally checked out the last customer for now. So, I go to work on finishing the new window display. The theme is *There's 'Snow" Place Like a Bookstore.* The main office sent paper snowflakes made from the pages of books. Yesterday Houston built two snow-people and a tree from stacked books. Today, I just have to finish setting out the last few books we're highlighting this week.

"It looks very pretty," a female customer comments as she walks past.

"Thank you," I respond with a smile, feeling a sense of pride in my work.

Then, I snap a few pictures to put on the store's social media page.

Before I know it, it's almost closing time. I'm wiping the counter down when I hear someone behind me clear their throat. I spin around, and the rag flies from my hand, landing on Duke's shoulder.

"Oh my gosh. I'm so sorry," I exclaim as I reach out to grab the rag.

"I didn't mean to startle you," he says, grinning.

"It's okay," I respond, attempting to regain my composure. "Can I help you with something?"

"I know Aurora put you on the spot this morning, so I wanted to give you an out. You don't have to feel obligated to have me at your holiday celebration. You can tell her—"

"I don't feel obligated. I'm delighted you're going to be there," I interject, feeling genuinely pleased.

"You are?"

"I am."

"That's great. Well, I better be going," he says, gesturing toward the door. "I don't want to miss the bus." He smiles, and the adorable dimple on his cheek makes an appearance, nearly melting me on the spot.

"Have a good evening."

"You too, Percy," he replies warmly.

Percy

WORKING IN A SMALL town has its perks. One of those is the bookstore closes the day before Thanksgiving and doesn't reopen until Black Friday. It's a much-needed day off. I wouldn't have been able to concentrate anyway. Duke's going to be at my house in less than twenty-four hours. While I'm assembling the spiced pecan pie, I put my phone on speaker and I put my phone on speaker and videocall Aurora.

"Hey, Perc. What's up?" Aurora asks as she appears on the screen a bright smile on her face.

"I'm scared to death about tomorrow. What do I talk to him about?" I fidget with the edge of my napkin, nerves gnawing at me.

Aurora throws her head back and laughs. "Anything. Every-thing."

"I don't know anything about him other than he comes into the bookstore every day, and he works on a computer." My hands clench into fists on the table.

"That's a start. Ask him about his job," Aurora suggests, leaning in closer.

"Then what?" I exhale heavily, feeling overwhelmed.

"Remember that website I told you about? The one where Chris and I get our date boxes?" Aurora's eyes light up with excitement. "That Real Life Romance site."

"What does that have to do with talking to Duke?" I raise an eyebrow in confusion.

"They have a page called Re-Getting to Know You where there's a ton of random questions to re-get to know, or in this case, get to know someone." Aurora leans back in her chair, tapping her fingers on the table.

"That's for people who're dating, though." I furrow my brow, uncertain.

"It doesn't have to be. Just go through the questions and pick a few for tomorrow. Use them as conversation starters." Aurora nods decisively.

"Conversation starters?" My lips quirk into a hesitant smile.

"Ice breakers. Whatever you want to call them. There're some really fun questions. It'll help. Trust me," Aurora encourages.

"I don't think I have a choice." I chuckle nervously, feeling a bit more at ease.

"You're worrying too much. Everything'll be fine." Aurora flashes me an encouraging grin.

After we hang up, I put the pie in the oven and set the timer. While I wait, I grab my laptop and open a web browser. I have a silent debate over whether I should check out this romance site or not. In the end, I decide it can't hurt to look at the questions even if I don't use them, right?

Duke

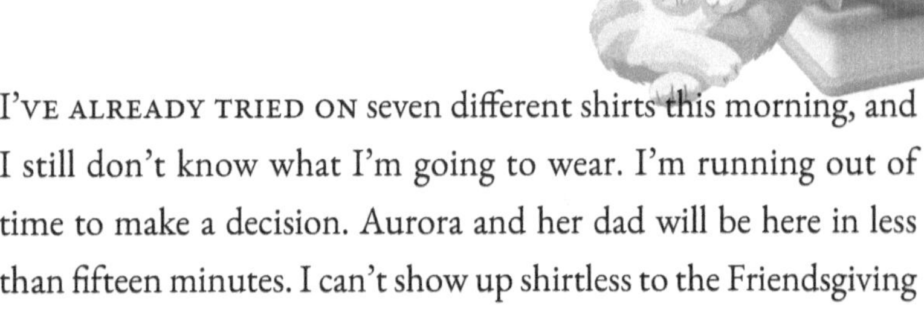

I'VE ALREADY TRIED ON seven different shirts this morning, and I still don't know what I'm going to wear. I'm running out of time to make a decision. Aurora and her dad will be here in less than fifteen minutes. I can't show up shirtless to the Friendsgiving dinner.

While I'm going through my shirts once more, my phone rings.

"Hello?" I say, answering the call.

"Hello dear," Mom responds warmly.

"I didn't expect to hear from you today," I admit.

"We wouldn't let the holiday pass without at least calling," she assures me.

I sit on the edge of my bed, phone pressed to my ear. "How's your vacation so far?" I inquire.

"It's incredible," Mom gushes. "We're docked in Bermuda right now. The islands are so beautiful."

"You really should plan a trip out here," Dad suggests.

As if I have time for a vacation.

"I'm glad you're having a good time," I say genuinely.

"I hope we didn't interrupt your holiday," Mom adds.

"Not at all. I'm at home," I assure her.

"I thought you were spending the day with friends?" Dad asks.

"I am," I confirm.

A car horn honks outside, breaking our conversation, and I rise to look out my bedroom window.

"I hate to cut this short, but my ride's here. I have to go," I explain.

"Have a wonderful holiday," Mom bids farewell.

"You, too," I reply before ending the call.

My parents sound relaxed and carefree. Unlike myself, who's still in the middle of a crisis. Knowing I've run out of time, I close my eyes and grab. When I open them, I'm holding a sage green polo. I pull it over my head and, with a last check in the mirror, go downstairs.

Yesterday, I asked Aurora what I could bring. She told me I didn't have to bring anything, but I didn't want to show up empty-handed. However, in addition to not being handy around the house, I also have zero cooking skills. So, I decided to bring the wine—pink, red, and white. I realize it may be overkill, but I don't know what anyone likes.

With my package in hand, I head out the door to my first Friendsgiving celebration.

I climb into the backseat of Aurora's car.

"Happy Thanksgiving," Aurora chirps with her usual enthusiasm.

"Same to you," I reply with a smile.

"Duke, this is my father, Earl. Dad, this is my friend, Duke."

"Nice to meet you, sir," I offer politely.

"Earl, please. And same to you," he replies, glancing at me through the rearview mirror with a friendly nod.

It's a short ride across town to Percy's house. But in that time, Earl peppers me with a myriad of questions about my family, my employment, and how I ended up in Washington. Now I know where Aurora gets her chattiness from.

Earl parks the car in front of a charming two-story home that is quintessentially Georgia. There're several rocking chairs on a wraparound porch and beautiful potted flowers hanging above the railings.

"Is this Percy's house?" After the question leaves my lips, I realize how dumb it must sound. Of course, this is her house, or we wouldn't be getting out of the car.

"It is," Aurora says as she walks around the car. "It's where she grew up. After her dad died—"

"Her father died?"

"Yeah, about eleven years ago. He had a heart attack."

"Does her mom live here with her?" I ask as we walk up the brick pathway leading to her front door.

"No." Aurora shakes her head. "Percy's mom left when she was a little girl."

"Oh."

Before we get to knock, the front door swings open.

"Happy Thanksgiving," Percy says with a big smile on her face.

"Happy Thanksgiving, doll." Earl wraps her in a bear hug.

"Everything smells delicious," Aurora says. "I'm starving."

"Good. Because I made enough for an army." The girls share a laugh before Percy looks at me. "Hi, Duke. I'm glad you could make it."

"I brought wine." I hold up the bag.

I brought wine. How about *hello* or *thanks for inviting me?* But no, I manage. *I brought the wine.* Nothing like sticking your foot in your mouth—as usual.

"Thank you." She steps aside. "Come on in."

I step inside Percy's house and am struck by how beautiful it is. The foyer is a spacious area with what looks to be original hardwood flooring. To my right is a majestic oak staircase. To my left is an impressive library with a fireplace and built-in bookshelves. I follow the trio into an expansive kitchen, which is a tasteful mix of modern and farmhouse.

"I can take those from you," Percy says.

"Thank you." I pass her the paper bag. "Your home is beautiful."

Her smile fades. "My dad did all the work himself. He always wanted a large family, but that wasn't in the cards."

"Why don't you come with me. We'll put the game on while the girls finish up," Earl says as we make our way through the kitchen. "Every year, I tell them I'd be fine with a paper plate on the couch. But they insist on this fancy dinner in the dining room." He motions to a formal dining area that appears set for dinner.

The kitchen opens to a great room where the focal point is a natural stone fireplace situated in the far corner. The ceiling opens to the second floor, where there appears to be a loft area. The back wall has a set of French doors flanked on each side by windows. Percy's father was clearly a very talented man.

Earl grabs a remote and sits on a recliner.

"Do you like football, Duke?" Earl inquires.

"I've never watched a game," I admit as I settle onto the leather sofa.

"Never?" Earl's eyebrows shoot up in surprise.

"No. My folks weren't into sports," I explain.

"Well, let me explain how the game works," he offers, clearly eager to share his knowledge.

Percy

Duke follows Earl into the living room while I put the wine in the fridge. It was very sweet of him to bring something. I didn't expect it.

"Did you go on the Real Life Romance site?" Aurora asks quietly.

"I did. But I don't think it's going to work." You can give the girl something to talk about, but you can't make her any less awkward saying it.

"Just be casual about it."

"Casual. Got it." I shake my head.

The oven timer goes off. I grab my oven mitts and pull the tray of dinner rolls out. While I arrange them in a basket, Aurora carries the platters from the warming drawer to the dining table. While we're getting all the food out, the doorbell rings.

"You're just in time," I say as I let my guests in.

Houston's mom, Laura, gives me a hug. "It's so nice to see you, honey."

"Dinner's ready," Aurora calls.

Everyone takes their seats around the table. Duke sits across from me, and I doubt that I'll be able to eat without getting distracted by his handsome face or his hazel eyes.

"Okay, you girls know the drill," Earl says. "Who's going first?"

"I will," Aurora says quickly. "I'm thankful that Chris will be home in a few weeks."

Earl smiles at his daughter. "Anything else?"

"That we're all able to be here together. We really should do this more often."

There's a chorus of agreement.

"I'll go next," Houston says. "I'm thankful for Percy's cooking and her company. I always look forward to it." He smiles at me.

I give a quick smile in return, then take my turn.

"I'm thankful all of you have become my second family and that none of us have to be alone during the holidays." I stop before I get too emotional. When I look across the table, I find Duke watching me intently.

We finish our thankful statements, and after Earl says grace, we start filling our dishes. The room is filled with conversation and laughter. Something it feels like this house is often missing, with it being just my cats and me. The cats, who, by the way, are all under the table winding themselves around the legs of my guests. Tess seems particularly interested in Duke.

After dinner, Laura, Aurora, and I clear the table.

"Thank you for your help. Why don't you two go outside with everyone else? I'll load the dishwasher."

"I hate leaving you with all these dishes," Laura voices her concern.

"I don't mind. It'll only take a few minutes," I assure her.

As the ladies join the men on the patio, I begin loading the dishwasher.

"Can I help?" Duke's voice startles me from behind.

"I've got it," I respond, a bit surprised.

"You did all the cooking. Helping with the dishes is the least I can do," he insists.

"If you insist," I acquiesce, rinsing the dishes and passing them to Duke, who carefully loads them into the machine.

"So, do you believe in Bigfoot?" I blurt out, the question catching me off guard.

Duke freezes with a plate in his hand.

Percy, what in the world? Bigfoot? Really? I can feel my cheeks heat from embarrassment.

"I've never thought about it," Duke says, resuming his task. "I mean, I've never led an expedition to find him, but I suppose I may be a believer. What about you?"

"Just because I've never seen something doesn't mean it's not real," I reply.

"Exactly."

We continue to work in silence. My heart is beating so loudly that I'm surprised Duke doesn't hear it. "What's your favorite book genre?" Duke asks.

"Romance," I respond with a smile. "I'm a sucker for a happily ever after. What about you?" This conversation thing isn't so hard after all.

"I don't get much time to read, but when I do, it's usually something tech-related," he admits.

"Would you ever jump out of a plane?" I blurt out another question from the website Aurora gave me.

"It's on my bucket list," Duke admits with a chuckle.

"Really? Why would you jump out of a perfectly good plane?"

My question makes him laugh. It's a beautiful, deep laugh. And that dimple, I've never seen it this close.

"What about you? Would you jump from a plane?"

Duke

Percy's questions are so random and unexpected. I feel myself falling for her more than I already have. I continue loading the silverware into the dishwasher while I wait for her answer.

"Well, I've never been on a plane."

"Never?" I ask, shocked.

She shakes her head. "Actually, I've not traveled very far out of Washington."

And with that statement, I decide I want to show her the world.

"Looks like we're done here," she says while drying her hands. "Thanks for the help."

"Anytime." I don't want this conversation to end.

"Why don't you give Duke the grand tour," Aurora suggests, causing me to jump slightly.

"I can do that. If you're interested in seeing the rest of the house, that is. It's just a house."

"I'd like that."

"Okay, follow me." I turn and lead the way back towards the foyer, Duke following close behind.

We walk back towards the foyer.

"Here's my library," Percy says, gesturing toward the room.

"I saw it on the way in. It's impressive," I remark.

"It's one of my favorite rooms in the house," she adds, smiling as she leads me further inside.

Next, she leads me up the steps. On the wall are pictures of an adorable little girl with long blonde braids.

"That's my dad and me," she says, her voice tinged with sadness.

"Aurora told me what happened. I'm very sorry. That must've been difficult," I respond, my heart aching for her.

She nods, tears shimmering in her eyes. "It was. Still is. Especially around the holidays. It was eleven years ago, but sometimes the hurt is so raw it feels like it was just yesterday."

Her words make me realize how lucky I am to still have both my parents.

Percy takes a deep breath and continues up the last few steps. We're standing in the loft area when I spot a desk with a laptop on it.

"Not much to see here, just my computer. Sorry about the mess." She gestures to a pile of containers. "It's all my Christmas decorations."

"I don't see a thing."

"Dad loved this area." She points to the two-story windows on the wall above the French doors. "Were his pride and joy. He loved to sit up here and watch the sunset."

I thought the windows were impressive from downstairs, but that was nothing compared to seeing them up here. The view of the setting sun casting hues of oranges across the sky is spectacular.

"It was a brilliant idea," I say.

"Ready for the rest of the tour?"

"Absolutely," I reply with enthusiasm.

We walk down a hallway, where she shows me two guest bedrooms.

"In here is the cat room," she says as we walk in.

On the walls are murals mimicking the outdoors, complete with green grass and flowers painted all along the baseboard. The ceiling is painted sky blue with white puffy clouds. There are several different cat climbing trees set up around the room and a toy box full of cat toys.

"Did you design it?"

"Aurora did all the sketches, and I helped her paint."

"You're both very talented."

I look around and spot three cats. A tuxedo cat is peeking its head out from an enclosed bed area. A black cat with a solid white face reminiscent of the Phantom of the Opera is perched high at the top. The three-legged tiger cat that kept my company through dinner walks between us and hops onto an empty perch. "What are their names?"

"The black one is Caspian. My tuxedo's name is Hemingway. And my tiger girl is Tess."

"Literary names?" I recognize the first two, but not Tess.

"Yes. Books and cats are my favorite things." She smiles.

We stay with the cats for a few minutes while Percy tells me about her plans to add some more features to the room, including a catwalk that Aurora's boyfriend is going to build when he gets home.

At the same time Percy turns toward the door, Caspian leaps from his perch, landing right in Percy's path. In an effort to not step on the feline, she loses her balance and falls right into my arms.

"Are you okay?" I ask, my arms on her shoulders, ensuring she's steady before I let her go.

"I am." She bites her lip before giving me a small smile.

She leads me out of the room to a set of doors at the end of the hall.

"The last room is just my bedroom."

We walk through the double doors, and my jaw drops. Her bedroom is the size of my entire Manhattan apartment. Not only is there an ensuite bathroom and a closet as big as my current bedroom, but there's also a large sitting area and another fireplace.

"I'm jealous of all your space," I admit, a pang of envy hitting me. Whether in the city or here, I've always lived in an apartment. It must be really nice to have your own house.

"It gets pretty lonely," she confides.

"I'm sorry for being insensitive," I quickly apologize.

"Oh no, you didn't say anything wrong," she reassures me. "It's a great house, but it can be a lot for one person to keep up with. Especially outside."

We both look out the windows that overlook the backyard. From here, I can see an expansive patio where everyone's gathered by a fireplace. Off the concrete area is a huge fenced-in yard. It must be at least a few acres.

"If you ever need help, just give me a call. I'd be more than happy to come over and give you a hand," I offer sincerely.

"Really?" Percy's eyes widen in surprise.

"I mean, I've never had a yard, so you'd have to teach me what to do," I admit with a chuckle.

"Never had a yard?" Percy tilts her head, a look of disbelief on her face.

"There aren't many places with grass in Manhattan, and Mrs. Custis only has a small property that she has the young boys from next door take care of," I explain.

"That makes sense."

"Are you ready for dessert?" Houston asks from the doorway, interrupting our conversation.

"I was just showing Duke around." Percy starts walking toward the door, and I follow. "We're on our way now."

"Not a problem. I just couldn't wait any longer to dig into your pies," Houston says, eyeing the desserts eagerly. He looks at me. "Percy makes the best pies I've ever tasted."

"I can't wait to try them," I reply, genuine excitement in my voice.

Percy

IT REALLY FELT LIKE Duke and I were starting to connect with each other. That is until Houston interrupted, asking about dessert. Now, we're back in the kitchen cutting the pies while everyone joins Houston bragging about my baking.

"Where did you learn to cook?"

"Trial by fire, I guess you'd say."

"She's going to make a wonderful wife one day," Houston says, putting his arm around me.

"Yeah. Okay." I laugh. "Why don't you carry this outside?" I give Houston the apple pie. "Here's one for you, too." Duke carries the pumpkin pie out.

After two more trips, where we bring out a chocolate cream pie, lemon meringue pie, and the spiced pecan pie, we gather at the outside table. Aurora pours everyone some wine, and I pass out plates full of dessert. Then, I walk back into the house to wash off the knife.

"Got a second?" Houston asks.

"Sure. What's up?"

"Let's go in here." He takes my hand and leads me into the library. "I've been wanting to ask you this for a while now." He shuffles his feet. "Now that I'm here doing it, I'm not sure how to say it."

"We talk all the time. There's nothing to be nervous about." Although I'm feeling super nervous right now, too, and I don't know why.

"Okay. Here goes. I really like you. A lot." He takes a step closer. "I'd like to take you out on a date. More than one date, actually. I'd like to call you my girlfriend."

He leans in, and oh my gosh, I think he's going to kiss me. I put my hands up, stopping him.

Mercury must be in retrograde or some other odd happening because I certainly didn't just get asked on a date by Houston. But by the way, he's staring at me, a hopeful expression on his face. It's clear he did ask and is waiting for an answer.

"Wow. Houston. Um. I don't think our dating is a good idea," I blurt out, feeling a rush of nerves.

"Why not?" he asks, disappointment evident in his voice.

Think fast, Percy. "I have a strict rule of not dating co-workers."

"Oh." Houston's shoulders slump, and he looks down briefly.

"I'm flattered you asked," I rush to add, hoping to soften the blow.

He's a really sweet guy. The kind any girl would be lucky to have as a boyfriend. But I don't see Houston as anything more than a friend.

"Doesn't hurt to ask, right?" He tries to play it off with a shrug.

"No, it doesn't." I force a smile.

"Can we pretend I never asked? I don't want things to be weird now."

"What never happened?" I reply with a smile, trying to ease the tension.

"Thanks, Perc," he says, appreciative of my understanding.

Duke

I walk into the house to use the guest bathroom and overhear Houston and Percy talking. I know I shouldn't eavesdrop, but I can't help myself. From where I'm standing, I can see their reflection in the mirror that hangs in the foyer. I can hardly believe what I'm hearing. He's just asked her out and is leaning in for a kiss.

What a fool I've been. Here I was, thinking Percy and I were connecting. That there was a spark between us. But I was so wrong—again. This whole time she was just being nice to me. Why? Because she felt sorry for me? I don't wait around to see what happens next. Instead, I backtrack quickly and go back outside, where I take my seat and resume eating my dessert. The pies really are the best I've ever tasted.

Several minutes later, Houston and Percy come back outside. She's laughing at something he's just said to her.

Once again, I'm too late, and the *other* guy gets the girl.

The rest of the evening, I find myself sitting quietly, wishing I could leave. My apartment isn't that far. I could walk. But if I left early, it would draw too much attention.

"What's wrong, Duke?" Aurora asks quietly as she walks by with some empty plates.

"Nothing. I'm just thinking about a website I'm building. It's giving me some issues." That's not entirely false.

"It's a holiday. You're not allowed to think about work." She takes the empty plate from my hand and brings it into the kitchen.

A short time later, Houston and Laura get up to say their good-byes.

"It was a pleasure to meet you, Duke. And nice to see you again, Earl." She smiles and starts laughing, drawing curious looks from everyone. "I'm sorry. Every time I look at you both, I can't help singing "Duke of Earl" to myself." Everyone joins her laughing.

It's another two hours before Earl says, "It's getting late. If we don't get going, this old man's gonna turn into a pumpkin."

"It's just you and Duke leaving. I'm spending the night here, remember?"

"Sure do, sweetpea." Earl kisses his daughter on the forehead. "You two girls have fun. And thank you again for dinner." He holds up the take-home container of food.

"Are you sure you don't want any leftovers, Duke?" Percy asks.

"I'm good. Thank you." After I say it, I see the hurt look in her eyes. "On second thought, I'd love some."

"Great." She hands me a container she already had made up. "Thanks for coming."

The girls wave goodbye as we walk down the brick pathway and get into the car.

We don't get to the end of the block before Earl says, "Pardon me if I'm overstepping. But I sense some chemistry between you and Percy."

His words shock me, and I don't know how to respond.

"Percy's like a second daughter to me. She's been through a lot."

"Sir, I—"

"Let me finish," Earl interrupts. "Her mom leaving was hard. Then, a few years later, her dad died in front of her. Well, that's more than any kid should have to go through. She's been alone for a long time. But you make her smile. Be gentle with her is all I ask."

"Yes, sir." I don't argue with the man. He clearly cares about Percy, but what he doesn't realize is it's not me she's interested in.

Percy

After Earl and Duke leave, I walk into the living room and flop down on the leather sofa.

"What's wrong?" Aurora asks as she drops down next to me.

"Houston asked me out."

"What?" She sits up so fast I'm afraid she's going to get whiplash.

"I was floored, too."

"What did you say?"

"I told him I don't date co-workers."

"I feel kinda bad for him." She sits back again. "There aren't too many young people here to choose from."

"Young being the keyword."

"You're not exactly an old maid." Aurora laughs.

"I'm going to be thirty in a few months. Houston's only in his early twenties. People would call me a jaguar." My comment makes Aurora laugh even harder. "What's so funny?"

"I think you meant cougar."

"Jaguar. Cougar." I wave my hand. "They're all big cats. Anyway, he's not the guy I'd like to go out with."

"Speaking of Duke, you two were quite chatty today. Why don't you just ask him out already?"

"Talking to him and asking him on a date are two *very* different things."

"I'm aware of that, but I think you should go for it. What's the worst that could happen?"

"He could say no."

"Any man who answered if he believes in bigfoot or not with a straight face isn't going to say no."

"You heard that?" I cover my face with my hands.

"I was coming in to grab my glass. I nearly dropped it when I heard that question. Where in the world—" Aurora laughs so hard tears are rolling down her face.

"I got it from that Real Life Romance website you sent me to." I slap her arm.

"Really?" She attempts to compose herself. "Well, he answered it and kept talking to you. So, I guess they know what they're doing."

Aurora and I spend the rest of the evening watching Christmas movies in our pajamas.

When we finally fall asleep, I dream about Duke. It's a world where I have the courage to ask him out. We fall madly in love with each other and live happily ever after.

His One, Her Only Publishing

To: M. Loveless

I wanted to let you know we received the signed pages back. Thank you very much for getting them back to us so quickly. I'm pleased to tell you that they sold out within twenty-four hours of the pre-orders going live.

Considering the high demand for signed copies of your books, I'd be remiss if I didn't ask you to reconsider your stance on doing a book tour. I understand your initial hesitation, but I can't stress enough how important doing this will be. Readers are desperate to get their hands on books with your autograph. I'm sure a book tour would be a huge success.

Once again, I've attached the sample schedule. Please think about what I've said while you take another look at it. Ideally, I would like to get it underway as soon as possible.

Warmest Regards,

Madeliene Bennet

Publicity Executive

Duke

I REALLY THOUGHT THINGS were going well. Percy and I were finally talking. And those questions she asked me. Do I believe in Bigfoot? Would I ever jump from a plane? As soon as the words left her lips, she had me under her spell. Those certainly weren't the standard *what's your favorite food* or *what's your favorite color?* They were fun and quirky—just like Percy.

When I saw her walk into the house alone, I decided that was the sign I was waiting for. I was going to take the chance and ask her out. Seize the day and all that. So, I gave her a minute and then followed in behind her.

What I didn't realize was that Houston was in the house. Not just in the house—he was with Percy. As I stood outside the library listening to their conversation, everything began to move in slow motion. Houston got there before me. He was about to kiss her. I couldn't stay and watch it happen, so I hurried out of the house.

I walk into my empty house and sit on my couch, putting my head back. I can't believe I let myself believe, even for a second, that somehow my luck had changed, and I could have a girl like Percy. I allowed myself to get caught up in the illusion that guys like me could get that girl. Unfortunately, that only happens in the movies.

In real life, the ordinary guy never gets the girl. Instead, we watch the *other* guy ride off into the sunset with the princess. Why did I let myself believe, even for a minute, that things would be different this time?

I didn't go to the café or the bookstore on Black Friday. I wasn't ready to see Percy with Houston or to answer any of Aurora's questions. Instead, I went to The Pig and Bull Grill, a yummy little restaurant in town, where I was able to both avoid the girls and finish up some projects.

But now, it's Monday again, and I can't avoid Nooks with Books any longer.

"How are you this morning, Duke?" Harold asks when I step onto the bus.

"I'm okay." Instead of taking the seat behind him, I sit across the aisle.

"How was your holiday?" he asks.

"It was okay."

He stops at the next stop and gives a double take when he notices I'm not in my usual seat behind him. "Everything alright?"

"I'm just trying something new today."

"And here I thought that practice was something reserved for the new year." Harold chuckles.

"Never too early to get started." I shrug.

The bus finally pulls up to my stop. "Have a good afternoon. I'll see you later."

"You too, Duke."

I check my watch. Percy usually runs late in the morning. She should be here in precisely ten minutes. I really don't want to be in the café when she gets there, so I take a stroll down the street and pop in Poss Ace Hardware for a look-see. I meander up and down the aisles, looking for nothing in particular. I'm not handy with do-it-yourself kinda things. Give me a computer that isn't working or pretty much any other electronic device, and I'm good. I can fix it, alter it, or build it from parts and pieces. But give me saws, hammers, or drills, and I'm way out of my league. People who can do this kind of work have my respect.

Twenty minutes later, I've walked each aisle twice and decide to chance leaving the hardware store to go to the café for breakfast. As I approach Nooks with Books, I peer into the window and spot Percy setting up a new book display. She's wearing a pink ruffly skirt with polka dot tights, and it looks like a sweater with candy canes on it. I don't want to get caught watching. So, while her back is to me, I walk past the store and into the café.

"Good morning, Duke. You're late today," Aurora greets me.

"I'm changing my schedule up a bit. You know, to keep things fresh." I set my bag down, not at my usual table to solidify my story, before heading to the counter to get my breakfast.

The microwave dings, and Aurora takes out a Triple Berry Muffin. "Are you changing up your usual order too?"

"Nope." I smile and take the offered muffin. "Some things will never change." I'm just sitting down when Pippi prances over, rubbing herself against my legs. "Good morning, beautiful." I reach down and scratch behind her ears.

Just as Aurora hands me my glass of tea, the bells on the door jingle. A man walks in with a cat carrier in each hand. "Special delivery," he announces.

"I'm sorry I can't sit and chat today. I have to get these new rescues settled in."

"Not a problem. Pippi and I will keep each other company."

"Thanks for understanding." Aurora turns to the man. "Let's take them into the back room." She leads the man into the cat's playroom, leaving Pippi and me in the quiet café.

I take more than my usual time eating breakfast and sipping on my tea while I scroll and re-scroll through the day's news stories. I go so far as to order another tea since I've been occupying the café for so long.

When Aurora brings it over, she sits across from me.

"You ready to tell me what's on your mind?" she probes.

"Nothing, really," I deflect.

She tilts her head and studies me for a minute. "You never stay this long."

"I'm sorry." I begin cleaning up my stuff. "I'll head out."

"That's not what I meant. You're more than welcome to stay as long as you want. You're just usually in a hurry to get next door," she observes, raising her eyebrows.

I shrug. "Like I said. Just trying to change things up a bit."

"Mhm," she acknowledges, taking my plate and empty cup, clearly not buying my story.

I wait until Aurora's out of listening distance before I speak softly to the ginger cat lying on my lap. "I have to get going. I'm already drawing too much attention."

Regretfully, I lift the cat and set her down on the floor. She meows loudly and makes a show of stretching before she walks away.

I grab my things, say goodbye to Aurora, and walk out the door.

Percy

IT's WELL PAST TIME for Duke to be at the store, but there's still no sign of him. I'm starting to get worried that something's wrong. There's only one other person who might have answers. This is going to look really desperate.

I may not know much about Duke, but the one thing I know is he always sticks to a schedule. Honestly, I was surprised he wasn't here Friday. I figured he was just trying to avoid the crowds because it was the biggest shopping day of the year. It would've been hard to get any quiet time to get work done. But trying something new seems very out of character.

Aurora:

He seems a bit off, but I haven't had a chance to talk to him. A few new rescues arrived, and I'm trying to get them settled in.

Percy:

Go take care of your kitties. TTYL.

At least I know he's okay, and he'll be in soon.

The questions from that Real Life Romance site seemed to work so well on Thanksgiving that I returned to the site over the weekend and found a few more questions. I even found a date idea. I decided to take the leap and ask him if he wanted to go out. The plan was to ask him before there were too many customers in the store. But since *he* never got here, I need to rethink my strategy.

I'm in the middle of waiting on a customer when the door opens. I look up like I always do to greet the incoming shopper and see its finally Duke. I give him a bright smile, but he doesn't even look up. Instead, he hurries across the store to the sitting area, and unlike normal, he sits with his back to the store's floor. That's really unlike him.

"Thanks for shopping at Nooks with Books," I say, bringing my attention back to the customer in front of me. "Have a great afternoon."

"You, too." The customer takes the reusable bag we just started offering and walks toward the door.

It seems like the line has died down for now, so I slide the bell onto the counter in case a customer needs assistance while I'm on the floor. We received a bunch of new inventory for the holiday shopping season that needs to be put on the shelves. Houston and I have been trying to get everything out as fast as possible.

All morning, I've been trying to set up the new M. Loveless display. The author has a new book coming out in a few weeks. With their immense popularity, we're showcasing their entire backlist throughout the store. It just so happens that the display I was in the middle of setting up is right next to the table where Duke is sitting. Since he's facing the wrong direction, I have to take a roundabout way to get there.

It's now or never.

With a deep breath, I approach his table, expecting to get some sort of reaction from him. Except when I get there, Duke doesn't even bother to look up.

"Hi," I say, giving a casual wave to draw his attention my way.

He returns it with a curt nod.

"How was your weekend?"

He makes a show of removing one of his earbuds. "What was that?"

"I asked how your weekend was," I repeat patiently.

"Fine," he replies tersely.

Okay, one-word answers. This isn't unfolding as I'd hoped.

"I have a bunch of work I need to get done," Duke gestures towards his laptop, his movements fluid.

"I'm sorry. I'll let you get back to what you're doing," I concede with a slight sigh.

"Mhm," he mumbles, seamlessly slotting the earbud back in, his focus returning to his tasks.

My hopes and mood just took a nosedive. What happened to the sweet, fun guy that was at my house last week? Maybe he's having a bad day? Everyone has those gray sky, glass half-empty kinda days. I shrug, trying not to overthink it, and get back to work.

The store is so busy today that before I realize it, half the after-noon's gone by. My phone's been buzzing away in my pocket. When I pull it out, I see why. It's twenty minutes past my lunch break, and I promised Aurora I'd meet her at her café for lunch today.

"I'm going next door for lunch," I inform Houston, who's in the midst of ringing out customers. "If it gets busy and you need me to come back early, just text."

"No problem. Have fun," Houston replies with a warm smile.

Although we agreed not to let things get weird after Houston asked me out last week, I was afraid it wasn't going to be that easy. Thankfully, it seems like everything's back to normal. Something I'm glad about. We work together a lot, and he's a good friend. I don't want anything to mess that up.

"Sorry I'm late," I say as I walk into the café.

"I'll be there in a minute," Aurora calls from her kitchen when I walk into the café.

"Take your time."

I set my lunch bag on the table and pop into the playroom to give the kitties some love while Aurora's finishing up in the kitchen.

I'm sitting in the middle of the floor when Aurora walks in. Pippi's laying in my lap, purring. Several cats, who are new arrivals, take turns getting pets.

"Are you auditioning for a Disney princess role?" Aurora teases, her laughter filling the air. "All you need is some birds and chipmunks to complete the scene."

"Very funny," I try to maintain a serious expression, but a laugh escapes anyway. "I can't help it if they all love me."

"I just took some new vegan cookies out of the oven. You want to be the first to try them?"

"Sorry, girl," I say as I carefully lift Pippi from my lap and stand up. "When did you start making cookies?"

"Today. I thought I'd try to add some for the holidays."

"Brilliant," I remark as we walk out of the playroom together, spotting the plate of cookies on the counter. "Peanut Butter? My favorite."

"I knew you'd be happy," Aurora says with a grin.

I grab one of the still-warm cookies and take a bite. It's the perfect combination of soft and chewy. "This is the best cookie I've ever tasted."

"Yay." Aurora claps her hands. "I was hoping you'd say that."

While we eat, Aurora fills me in on all the things she's hoping to do to expand her business over the holidays. She also tells me about the website Duke's building for her.

"I knew you were looking for a website. But I had no idea about the muffin and cookie mixes." Aurora's always been super creative. It wouldn't surprise me to see her succeed in making her brand go nationwide.

"Enough about me. I'm dying to hear what happened with Duke." Aurora watches me expectantly.

Over the weekend, I told Aurora my plans. Which, of course, she supported wholeheartedly. Unfortunately, she's about to be as disappointed as me.

"I didn't ask him."

"Why not?"

"I tried to talk to him, but he blew me off. He said he was busy and couldn't talk."

"Hmm." Aurora takes the last bite of her sandwich. "Maybe he has a deadline coming up or something." She pushes her chair out and walks behind the counter. "I have an idea."

Duke

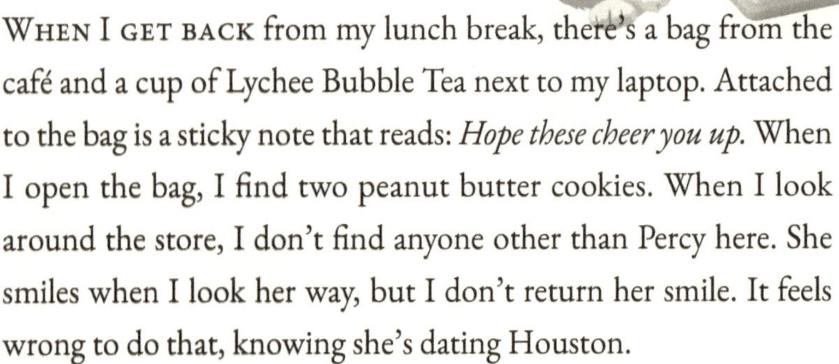

When I get back from my lunch break, there's a bag from the café and a cup of Lychee Bubble Tea next to my laptop. Attached to the bag is a sticky note that reads: *Hope these cheer you up.* When I open the bag, I find two peanut butter cookies. When I look around the store, I don't find anyone other than Percy here. She smiles when I look her way, but I don't return her smile. It feels wrong to do that, knowing she's dating Houston.

I'm unsure how to deal with the awkwardness I'm feeling regarding Percy. I hate even the thought of it, but I may have to find a new place to work. Knowing how I feel about Percy, it's going to be too hard watching her every day, knowing she's off-limits.

I've never been one to rush into a decision. So, I give myself until the end of the week to make a decision about where to work. What I do know for now is that I don't want to linger when it's close to closing time. While Percy's waiting on a customer, I sneak out and head over to the café.

Aurora has offered to let me stay in the café to work. After I show her the website, I'll ask if the offer still stands. That will at least give me some options to consider.

"Hey, Duke. You here for your muffin?" Aurora's voice calls out from behind the counter.

"I am. And I'll take some more of those cookies if you have them. Peanut butter cookies are my favorite."

"Percy was excited to bring them to you."

Percy? Why would she do that? Shouldn't she be bringing treats to her boyfriend, not me?

"Do you have a few minutes?"

"Sure. What's up?" Duke responds, his tone casual.

"I finished your website. I was hoping to give you a tour of it so you can let me know what changes you want made before it goes live."

"I wasn't expecting it to be done so fast," she says as she comes to sit down.

Here goes nothing. I usually do this with clients over a video conference. It's nerve-wracking with my client sitting across the table from me. I turn the laptop to face her and slide my chair over so I can see the screen to explain everything to her.

We go over the main pages for the café itself. I included photos I snapped inside the café. We also review the online menu to ensure everything's correct. Lastly, I show her the online shop.

"I especially love that you were able to take the colors from the actual cafe. How did you do it?" Aurora admires the website, curiosity sparking in her eyes.

"That was easy. I took a few pictures and color-matched them in my design program," Duke explains, his tone matter-of-fact.

Next, we move to the adoption pages. Each cat has a complete bio and a few pictures that I hope will help their individual personalities shine.

"All prospective adoptees have to do is click the paw print, and they'll be brought to the adoption application. Once it's complete, it'll show up in your email inbox."

"You took my vision and made it a reality," Aurora says, swiping at a tear. "I can't thank you enough."

"No thanks necessary. It was my pleasure," Duke responds warmly.

"Now," she says and raises an eyebrow. "You mentioned a barter. What did you have in mind?"

"Actually, I changed my mind on that," Duke admits.

"Oh. You want me to pay for the website instead?" Aurora's brow furrows with concern.

"No. I mean, what I wanted to ask isn't a thing anymore," Duke explains.

"Did it have anything to do with Percy, by any chance?" Aurora asks, her tone curious.

Am I that obvious? "It did. But it doesn't matter now," Duke admits reluctantly.

"Why not?" Aurora presses, her curiosity piqued.

"She's dating Houston."

"Dating Houston?" Aurora looks at me as if I've grown a second head. "Where did you get an idea like that?"

Aurora listens intently while I explain what I saw and heard on Thanksgiving.

After I finish my story, she says, "Percy isn't dating Houston. You must've left before you heard her turn him down."

"She turned him down?" I repeat, ensuring what I heard was correct.

"She did," Aurora confirms with a nod.

This information changes everything. Percy's not in a relationship. Is it too much to hope I still have a shot?

"So." Aurora grins. "Is the barter back on?"

I chew my lip. Indecision and nerves are getting the best of me. It's been a very long time since I've asked a woman out. Memories of the humiliation I suffered in my last relationship push to the surface. I really want to ask Percy out. But is it worth the possible embarrassment of her turning me down? Or is it better to live with the dream of what if, never knowing what her answer would be? Allowing myself to live in a dream where Percy and I, as a couple, always remains a possibility.

But maybe this is the time when the good guy gets the girl. If I don't take Aurora up on her offer to help, I could end up missing the best thing that's ever come into my life.

It's now or never, Duke.

"It's on," I declare, though with a hint of uncertainty. "I haven't dated in quite some time, though. Do you have any pointers?"

"May I?" Aurora gestures to my laptop.

"Sure," I respond, pushing it closer to her, though I'm not really sure where she's going with this.

Aurora's fingers fly across the keyboard. When she's done, she turns the screen to face me.

"I love this website. They have all sorts of date ideas."

"Real Life Romance?" I inquire as I read the information on the landing page. "This has to be a gimmick."

"It's the real deal. Chris and I use it all the time," Aurora assures me.

I scroll through the pages. Re-getting to know you. Do-it-your-self-dates, Pre-made date boxes. Curiosity gets the best of me, and I decide to look closer at the do-it-yourself dates.

To my surprise, I find some intriguing date starters. The Scavenger Hunt Date grabs my attention, and I click on it for more details. While it seems sweet and fun, I can't help but feel that Percy deserves something more unique and memorable than a pre-packaged date. "I don't know. It seems like I'm cheating if I take this and copy it."

"It's not cheating," Aurora asserts, tapping her finger on the table. "How about you take the spirit of the idea and make it personal?"

That was all the encouragement I needed. "I've got it." I close the laptop and stuff it into my messenger bag. "You're the best." Grabbing my things, I rush toward the door.

"Duke," she calls, dangling a bag. "You forgot these."

"Thanks."

"Anytime." Her voice carries a warmth that makes me smile as I head out.

Percy 

PERCY: I DON'T KNOW what's wrong with him. He was acting like Dr. Jekyll and Mr. Hyde.

I'm so disappointed. I'd finally worked up the courage to ask Duke if he wanted to go on a date. But when I tried to talk to him, all I got was the cold shoulder.

Aurora:

> Cut him some slack. Maybe he just had a bad day.

Percy:

> I guess so.

Aurora:

> Don't read too much into it. Tomorrow's a new day. Clean slate and all that goodness.

I climb into bed, and my fur babies jump in with me, each taking their chosen spot. Caspian lays on the pillow next to my head. Tess curls up by my legs. And Hemmingway lies by my feet. I'm hoping I won't feel so glum after a good night's sleep. My eyes close, and I drift off to dreamland.

Aurora and I are sitting by the fountain in the Town's Square. We're minding our own business when a marching band comes out of nowhere. Leading the band is Aurora's dad, Earl. He's dressed like Gene Chandler from his album cover. Complete with the red vest, cape, cane, and top hat. He's singing the lyrics to the song "Duke of Earl." Coming up behind him is Duke, who's dancing to his very own beat. People begin coming out of the storefronts, cheering on the parade. The entire time, Aurora and I are frozen in place, watching the spectacle in front of us.

Despite the odd dreams that plagued me all night, I find myself no better in the morning. Even my favorite yellow top and blue skirt fail to lift my spirits.

"I'll see you three later," I say to the cats, who are sitting on the steps watching me as I walk out the door and head to work. As I approach the downtown area, I see the town workers putting up decorations in preparation for the upcoming holidays.

I pop into the café to grab my breakfast and am surprised to see Duke already there. When he sees me, he quickly looks at his phone. I guess he's still ignoring me today. I wish I knew what I did to upset him.

"Can I get these to go?" I inquire.

"You sure?" Aurora questions.

"I'm sure," I confirm.

Surprisingly, Aurora doesn't argue. She puts my muffin in a pink paper bag and hands me my tea.

"Thanks. I'll see you later," I say gratefully.

It might be childish, but I don't want to sit in the small café with *him*. I'll eat breakfast in my office and catch up on emails before the store opens. With the Christmas shopping season in full swing, we will surely be busy again. Actually, I'll be extra busy because Houston has this week off.

I'm trying to balance my tea and the muffin bag while digging in my bag, searching for the keys to the store, when something falls from the handle. Carefully, so I don't spill my tea, I reach down to pick up what appears to be a paper flower that, upon further inspection, is made from the pages of a book. It's even painted a pretty pink. Attached to it by a little ribbon is a note that reads:

I read the odd message twice, then glance around. I don't know what I expect to find, but there's no one who even seems to notice me standing here. With my paper flower in hand, I unlock the door and head straight to my office. Once I'm there, I text Aurora. Maybe she knows something.

Percy:

I found this on the door of the bookstore.

I attach a picture of the flower and the note. The chat bubbles dance on the screen almost immediately.

While I eat my muffin, I try to clear my inbox, but I find it hard to stay focused. My mind keeps drifting to the paper flower lying on my desk and the cryptic poem attached to it. I'm just as confused as before, but my time's up. It's time to open for the day.

When I unlock the door, several people are outside waiting to come in.

"Morning. Sorry to keep you waiting," I apologize as I finally open the door to the store, realizing I'm running late.

I step aside and let everyone into the store. While I'm helping a customer find a book, I notice Duke walking in. He looks right at me, but his face has no emotion. He walks past me without so much as a *good morning*.

Fortunately for me, the store is so packed today. Being here alone means I've had no time to think about the note or worry about Duke's weird behavior toward me.

I'm walking back to the register to ring out the customer I'm currently waiting on when I spot another flower. This one's painted purple. Curiosity begs me to ignore the person standing across the counter from me so I can read the note. I manage to ignore it—at least long enough to ring the customer out.

As soon as the customer walks away, I pick up the flower and read the attached note:

Whoever left this here couldn't have gotten very far. I was only in the aisle with the customer for a few minutes. I look around the store, but again, no one's watching me. Several customers are browsing the books on display. Duke is in the same position he's been in all day pn his laptop with his head down. Several other customers are sitting at tables and chairs, looking through books and magazines. Nothing looks suspicious, which only confuses me more. Someone has to be behind this.

Because I'm here alone today, I close the store down during my lunch break. "Follow my hunch," I mumble to myself as I lock the door. I got it—the café. I rush next door in search of my next clue and, if my *hunch* is correct, some answers from Aurora.

As soon as I walk in, I spot a cup of my favorite drink here, Banana Bubble Tea. Beside it, lying on the counter, is a yellow paper flower with another note attached. Before I get to the counter, Aurora appears from the kitchen.

"Start talking. Who's leaving these?" I hold up the flower.

"I don't know what you're talking about." She feigns innocence.

"You might've been able to get away with that this morning. But whoever it is had to have been in here. Who is it?"

"Don't know." She shrugs. "I guess you'll have to read the clue to find out."

I read the note aloud:

I take a sip of the cool drink. "I wish I was Nancy Drew. She'd already know who this mystery person is."

"Why don't you just enjoy whatever *this*—"She motions toward the flower. "Is. Someone's obviously trying to do something nice for you."

"I guess. But I can't imagine who." An idea pops into my head, and I set the tea down. "It isn't Houston, is it? Please tell me it's not him."

"I can neither confirm nor deny that." Aurora grins.

"Come on, you're supposed to be my best friend."

"And as your best friend, I'm telling you to play along. Let yourself have some fun for a change."

"Fine," I say and sit down to eat. "At the very least, I'm getting some pretty flowers to display at home. Hopefully, the cats won't eat them." I giggle.

"Guess what," Aurora says excitedly.

"What?"

"Chris is coming home Friday," she squeals.

"Oh my gosh. I'm so excited for you." This past year has been difficult because he's been deployed for so long.

"I have to close early on Friday to leave for Fort Gordon. Would you mind looking in on the cats before you go home?"

"Not at all."

"Thank you, Percy."

The door opens, and a few customers walk in.

"I'll be right there. Sorry, I can't stay with you. I've been crazy busy all day."

"It's fine. I'm almost done. The bookstore has been busy, too."

When I'm leaving, the line of waiting customers stretches almost to the door. I wave goodbye and make my way back to the store.

Percy

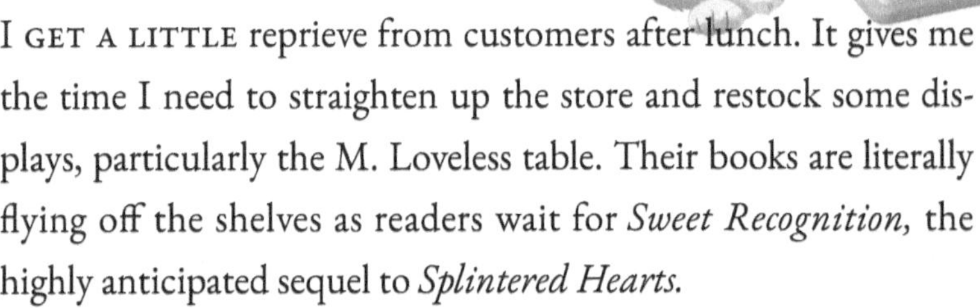

I GET A LITTLE reprieve from customers after lunch. It gives me the time I need to straighten up the store and restock some displays, particularly the M. Loveless table. Their books are literally flying off the shelves as readers wait for *Sweet Recognition,* the highly anticipated sequel to *Splintered Hearts.*

I walk over with an armload of paperbacks and notice Duke's things are gone. He must've taken them with him when he left for lunch. Makes sense with how many people have been in and out of here. But he also hasn't come back. I guess he really is trying to change things up.

If I had more courage, I'd approach him tomorrow and ask him what the heck is going on. What changed between Thanksgiving and yesterday? But let's face it, I'll never be the person who's able to speak her mind. That's why I'm alone and am forced to write about the fairy tale where the girl gets her prince.

Now, these notes are taking me on a possible wild goose chase. I have to trust Aurora knows what's going on since whoever this person is has been in the café. She wouldn't allow me to do anything where I'd knowingly get hurt. My job now is to play along and hopefully find my pot of gold at the end of the rainbow.

A turtle's pace doesn't come close to describing how slowly the clock moves for the remainder of the afternoon. In between customers, I read and re-read the notes, trying to analyze every word, hoping they contain some clue as to who they might be coming from. But I've come up with absolutely nothing.

After a final walk through the store to make sure everything is in its place, I'm finally locking the door for the evening. Then, I'm off to the fountain in the town square to search for my next clue. On my way across the street, I do my best to be aware of my surroundings, certain if I look hard enough, I'll discover the source of my scavenger hunt. I spot a mom corralling her children at the playground, presumably to go home after an afternoon of play, and several farmers at the market packing up their wares for the evening. Much to my disappointment, there's no one else around.

I walk all around the fountain, looking for a flower. It takes a bit, but I finally spot a red paper flower tied to a bench.

Knowing they'll be closing up for the day, I hurry to the end of the block, hoping I'm not too late.

I'm out of breath when I arrive, but I've made it just as they're starting to close up.

"I'm sorry to bother you. I know you're closing," I say apologetically.

"We were expecting you," Michele says with a smile. "I'll be right back."

She disappears into their back room. When she returns, she's holding a beautiful bouquet of flowers. Right away, I pick out lavender roses and pink chrysanthemums. Although the flowers are gorgeous, I'm a little disappointed that there's no paper flower or note.

"Do you happen to know who they're from?" I inquire, curious about the sender.

"I'm sorry. The order came in online and only had an address on it," Michele explains apologetically.

"Can you tell me the address?" I ask, hoping to track down the sender.

"I wish I could, but I'm unable to give out our customers' personal information," Michele replies regretfully.

"I understand. Have a good evening," I bid farewell politely.

"You too, Percy," Michele responds with a smile.

Once I'm back outside, I spot it—a lavender-painted paper flower nestled in the center of the bouquet. Someone had to be in to drop this off. I don't want to cause a scene by going back in and demanding to know who it was, though. Carefully, I pull the flower out, but there's no note. I'm about to give up hope when I spot a tiny end of a gold ribbon peeking out from the cellophane wrap.

Getting the note out without destroying the packaging takes a bit of work. I really should have waited until I got home, but I wanted to read it now to find my next clue.

I'm certain my next words will disappoint you. This bouquet of flowers is today's last clue. Get a good night's sleep. There's no need to weep. Tomorrow's a new day. More clues are certain to come your way.

"Tomorrow?" I blow out a frustrated breath. "How am I going to wait until tomorrow?" Whoever this person is clearly doesn't understand I'm not the most patient person when it comes to surprises.

Duke

AFTER AURORA TOLD ME Percy and Houston aren't dating, she also let me know that Percy's pretty miffed at me for ignoring her. I don't want to alert her that I'm behind the clues, so I've spent the week keeping up the ruse that I'm uninterested in talking to her. It's not been easy, especially when I see the hurt and confusion on her face. Everything will be revealed in a few days.

So far, my plan is working perfectly. Percy has no idea the flowers and clues are from me. I don't know where I'd be if Aurora hadn't agreed to help. It's taken both of us to get the flowers and clues placed without getting caught. I'd never be able to pull this off.

Over the next few days, Percy collects the paper flowers I've left all over town with notes attached to them all. The last message of each day has a small gift attached to it. The gifts are all clues for the date I'm hoping she says yes to going on.

Tuesday was the flowers. Wednesday was a small boat from On the Square Antiques and Gifts. Thursday was a journal and pen from Fievets. Friday was Percy's favorite sandwich, the 'Grown-up" Grilled Cheese from Maddy's Public House.

Tomorrow, Percy will receive the final clue revealing my identity. Fingers crossed she says yes.

His One, Her Only Publishing

To: M. Loveless

It's been over a week, and I haven't heard back from you. Have you given the book tour any more thought? With your new release set to come out on New Year's Day, I'm sure you understand time is of the essence.

Warmest Regards,

Madeliene Bennet

Publicity Executive

M. Loveless

To: Madeline Bennet

I apologize for the delay in getting back to you. With the holiday season upon us, I've been swamped. I've gone over the schedule again and considered your request. Although I'm still uncomfortable agreeing to a whole book tour, I am willing to make a concession.

Here's my proposition. Instead of agreeing to an entire tour, which would take precious time out of my writing schedule, how would you feel about doing a New Year's Eve early release party? I would agree to appear in person to sign copies of *Sweet Recognition*.

If the response is positive, I'll consider scheduling another special event.

I look forward to your thoughts.

Sincerely,

M. Loveless

His One, Her Only Publishing

To: M. Loveless

I think your idea is fantastic. You have no idea how pleased I am that you're agreeing to this.

Given the response I'm confident an event like this will receive, I think our flagship location in New York City would be a perfect venue.

I'll arrange for transportation and accommodations for you. Do you have a preference for hotels?

Warmest Regards,

Madeliene Bennet

Publicity Executive

M. Loveless

To: Madeline Bennet

I'm glad you like my idea. However, I don't see this event happening in New York City. I'd like this party to occur at Nooks with Books in Washington, Georgia.

Picture it, a sweet, southern small-town reminiscent of the one in the book. Readers will feel as though they are walking in the characters' footsteps. Washington has the same charm as the fictional town in *Splintered Hearts and Sweet Recognition.* And it should since Washington is the location I used as the inspiration for the story.

I'd love to see excerpts from the books used in the marketing campaign to introduce my readers to Washington. This town and its small businesses deserve the traffic an event like this might bring them.

It's imperative to me we have this event at this particular location. It holds a special place in my heart. I'm hoping you'll agree.

Sincerely,

M. Loveless

His One, Her Only Publishing

To: M. Loveless

That's certainly an unconventional request. However, given Washington's publicity after winning the Home Channel's contest last year, and with it being the inspiration for the setting of your novel, I must agree. Your idea to host this event in Washington, Georgia, is brilliant.

I've already contacted Janelle Graham, the district manager for Nooks with Books, to ensure they can accommodate our request. As you can imagine, she was ecstatic. She assures me the Washington store is the perfect place to host your first book signing.

The event information has been sent to our marketing department. We're focusing our manpower on getting the publicity for the signing out to the public as soon as possible.

I'm very excited and thankful you've decided to do this. I believe you will see precisely why events like this are important to your continued success.

I'll be in touch with more information as soon as it becomes available.

Warmest Regards,

Madeliene Bennet

Publicity Executive

Percy

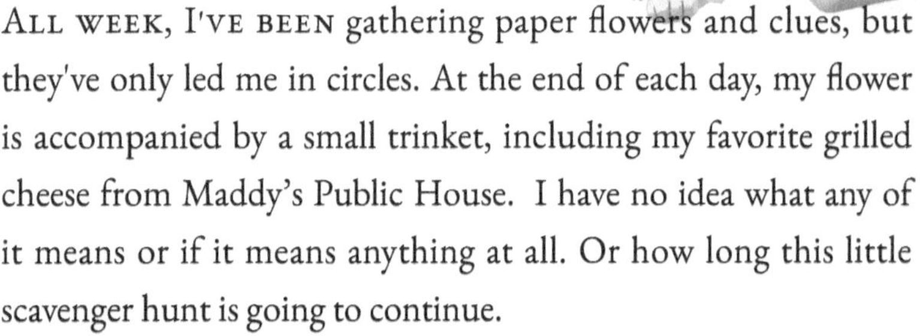

ALL WEEK, I'VE BEEN gathering paper flowers and clues, but they've only led me in circles. At the end of each day, my flower is accompanied by a small trinket, including my favorite grilled cheese from Maddy's Public House. I have no idea what any of it means or if it means anything at all. Or how long this little scavenger hunt is going to continue.

What's even more frustrating is Aurora knows more than she's letting on, but her lips are zipped. I have a sneaking suspicion she and Chris are behind this. They've been after me to meet several of his army buddies in the hopes of my striking a romance with one of them. I'll die if she comes home tomorrow with one of them.

Speaking of tomorrow, I'm so ready for a day off. Thankfully, the store's closed on Sundays because it's been super busy without Houston all week. Now that we've been open for a year and have a better idea of customer volume, I've emailed Janelle to ask about hiring some part-time associates to give us some relief.

I received a beautiful powder blue flower with my clue today. Like the first one, this flower was also on the handle of the store's door. The clue read.

I've had a fun week, hopefully putting a smile on your cheek. My poems may be cheesy, but I hope they haven't made you uneasy. One last clue you will receive. I hope it will help you to believe. All the clues you've had to seek every day this week. The last one will be different. The clue will come to you.

Excitement carried me through the day. Each time the door opened, I dropped what I was doing, hoping it was this mysterious clue I'd been promised. But the only deliveries that arrive are books for the store.

Five o'clock came and went a half hour ago. Even though the store's closed, I stay late just in case, but nothing arrives. It's like all the excitement of the past week has been building to this moment—the last clue. But when nothing happens, the bubble bursts.

Could this have all just been a prank? If Aurora didn't know who was behind these notes, I'd suspect that's the most likely case. But Aurora would never knowingly allow someone to get my hopes up and then just disappear.

It's funny, how just a few days ago, a *Secret Admirer* wasn't something I ever dreamed about. But after the excitement of finding these beautiful paper flowers and the notes all week, I found myself looking forward to what was next. That's all gone now. There is no more *next*. I lock up the store and start for home, surprised at how sad I'm feeling.

After I change into yoga pants and a T-shirt, I pull out the leftovers I planned to have for dinner tonight and put them in the oven. While my dinner cooks, I take a few minutes to feed the cats. I'm in the middle of filling their bowls when the doorbell rings. As I approach the door, I see a delivery person on the porch.

"Good evening. I'm looking for a Persephone Douglas," he says over the box he's holding.

"That's me." I smile and step aside, allowing him to bring the large box in. "You can put it on the bench."

"Can you sign here, please?" He holds out a clipboard he was balancing on top of the box, and I sign where he points. "Have a good night."

When I turn around, the cats are already on top of the box doing some exploring of their own. "How about I open it?" I shoo them off and tear at the tape that's holding the mysterious package closed. I'm not sure what I was expecting to be in it, but it isn't what I find. Inside is an old-fashioned-looking wicker picnic basket. An orange flower with a note is attached to the handle. After untying it, I read the note.

When I learned you felt rejected, I had to do something quite unexpected. I sent you on a chase that brought you all over the place. Each day ended with a clue, especially for you. This is the final gift. It requires you to act swift. Please keep the food cold so it doesn't grow mold. Tomorrow's the day I'd like to take you away. If you'll allow me this pleasure, it will be a day you will treasure. I'll pick you up at noon. I hope it comes soon. Text me your reply. Please don't say no,
or I'll cry.
~Duke 212.646.8315

Opening the basket, I find several different sandwiches, salads, and drinks. Everything that's needed for a picnic. I take the basket into the kitchen and, like the note directed, put the food in the refrigerator so it doesn't spoil. Then, I return to the note, reading it over several more times, convinced I must have misinterpreted it.

It can't possibly be, can it? I snap a picture and text Aurora.

Percy:

> I'm sorry to interrupt your homecoming. Hi Chris. But what does this say?

Aurora:

> What do you mean? LOL

Percy:

> I'm not sure what this says.

My phone rings.

"You didn't have to call," I mention casually.

"It's kinda hard to read to you over text," she explains.

"Does it say what I think it says?" I inquire, hoping for confirmation.

"I guess that depends on what you think it says?" she replies teasingly.

"I think it's Duke asking me on a date," I announce, feeling a mix of excitement and uncertainty.

"That's correct," she confirms with a chuckle.

"You knew about this?" I question, surprised.

"I did," she admits, still chuckling.

"I'm confused," I confess, taking a seat on a chair at the kitchen island and running my fingers over the wicker on the basket. "He hasn't spoken a word to me since Thanksgiving, yet he's asking me on a date?"

"He overheard Houston ask you out, but he didn't stick around to hear you turn him down," Aurora explains.

"That's why he was so upset Monday," I realize, everything beginning to make sense. "But why hasn't he talked to me all week?"

"He didn't want to give himself away, so he kept up the charade," Aurora clarifies.

My head is spinning. I don't know what to think or do.

"Perc? You there?" Aurora's voice brings me back to the conversation.

"I am. Sorry," I reply, feeling distracted.

"Did you text him yet?" Aurora asks, breaking the silence.

"No," I say quietly. "What do I say?"

"Being as though you've been wanting to go out with him for as long as he's wanted to go out with you, I'd assume you'd say yes," Aurora suggests.

"I'd like to say yes," I admit, feeling a rush of nervous excitement.

"Then get off the phone with me and text him," Aurora encourages.

"Okay," I agree, determination in my voice.

"We'll be home tomorrow evening. I expect to be told every detail," Aurora teases.

"Love you, Ror," I say affectionately.

"Love you too, Perc," Aurora replies with warmth.

After we hang up, I open a new message and type in Duke's number. My hands are shaking so much I can barely type. I set the phone on the counter as I try to compose myself.

Beep. Beep. Beep. The timer on the oven goes off, and I pull out my steaming meal.

"I'll text him after I finish eating," I say to Hemingway, who's sitting on the far side of the island, clearly judging me. "Fine. I'll do it now." She jumps down, seemingly satisfied with my answer.

Percy:

> I got my delivery.

Duke:

> I'm glad to hear it.

My heart is pounding. I've never done anything like this before. I haven't had a date since prom, and even that wasn't a *real* date. Aurora arranged for me to go with one of Chris's friends, Mark Morris. It was totally a pity thing, but he was sweet about it.

Duke:

> Have you decided on an answer?

Percy:

> I'd love to go out with you.

Duke:

> I'm glad to hear it. I wasn't sure after those silly poems if you'd still want to talk to me.

Percy:

> I thought they were adorable.

Duke:

> I'm no Shakespeare. But thank you.

Percy:

Where are we going tomorrow?

Duke:

That's my final surprise.

Percy:

Can I have a hint? So I know what to wear?

Duke:

Wear something suitable for an outside activity. I'll pick you up at noon.

Duke:

Don't forget the picnic basket. ;-)

The winky face emoji makes me laugh.

While I wash the dishes, I wrack my brain trying to figure out what Duke's planning. I assume it has something to do with the gifts I found at the end of every day. A boat, a journal, and a picnic. He said it's an outside activity, which makes the boat make sense. But other than that, I have no idea what it could be.

I drift off into sleep, my mind filled with dreams of what my first date might be like.

Duke

SHE SAID YES. I was sure after she read my ridiculous attempts at poetry, she'd think I was the biggest loser and would laugh in my face. But she didn't

That fact still feels as unbelievable this morning as it did last night when she texted me. All week, as she collected the flowers I made and the clues I left, I worried about her reaction. Insecurity plagued me at every turn, and I almost gave up a few times. But Aurora kept encouraging me to keep going. And I'm glad I did because right now, I'm getting into the rental car parked in front of my apartment to pick Percy up for our first date.

My legs feel like jelly as I exit the car and walk up to her house. I ring the bell and wait. When Percy opens the door, she steals my breath away. She's wearing a pair of rolled-up blue jeans that stop mid-calf and a blue button-down top tied in a knot at the bottom. In her hair is a red and white polka dot scarf. She resembles a modern Rosie Riveter.

"Hi," she says shyly, her voice barely above a whisper.

"You look great," I compliment, noticing the blush creeping up her cheeks.

"Thank you," she responds, her cheeks turning pink. "Would you like to come in?"

"Sure," I agree, returning her smile.

Percy opens the interior door further, and I step inside. In less than thirty seconds, her tiger cat bounds down the wooden staircase and begins rubbing herself against my leg.

"Hello again, Tess," I greet warmly as I bend down to pet the kitty. "It's nice to see you."

"She's typically shy around guests, but it seems as though you made a good impression on her the last time you were here," she remarks with a smile.

"I'm glad she feels comfortable with me," I reply, feeling pleased.

"I have to grab my shoes, and then I'll be ready to go," she informs me.

"Sounds great," I respond, eager to spend time together.

Tess jumps up and lies next to me. Cats often get a bad rap for being independent and lacking in affection. But it's my experience that they're more affectionate than many people give them credit for.

A few minutes later, Percy walks back down the steps. This time, wearing a pair of red sneakers. I stand up just as she gets to the bottom of her staircase.

"Ready to go?" I ask, glancing at her.

"I am," she replies, her smile lighting up the room.

I grab the picnic basket and give Tess a soft pat on the head. "It was nice seeing you again, girl." She meows and jumps from the bench.

After getting settled in the car, we start the drive to the top-secret location. I thought ahead and plugged the address into the GPS before I picked up Percy. I want to keep the element of surprise for as long as possible.

The radio plays some soft rock softly, but aside from that, we drive in silence. I sneak glances at Percy, who's watching the scenery pass out the window, her hands folded tightly in her lap.

"Do you believe in the monster under your bed?" It's my turn to shock her with a question from that romance website.

From the corner of my eye, I see her shift in her seat, so her body's angled toward mine. "Of course I do. You won't ever catch my feet hanging over the edge. Can never be too safe." She giggles.

"If you had a pet unicorn, what would you name it?" I inquire, curious.

"I'm guessing Aurora told you about the website, too," she responds with a chuckle.

"She did," I confirm.

"That's an easy one. I'd name it Serendipity. What about you?" she asks in return.

With that simple exchange, the tension melts away, and the conversation flows smoothly.

Percy

DUKE DIDN'T THINK I'D ask the question back. He crunches his forehead while he thinks about his answer.

"I got it. Stu," he says matter-of-factly.

I'll be the first to admit that I was skeptical when Aurora told me about that website. I mean, really, how could some random question generator actually help. But now that I've tried it, I'm a believer. Somehow, their crazy questions always seem to take the pressure off and make talking seem so much easier.

"All week, I've been trying to figure out what the gifts mean," I confess, hoping for some insight.

"Oh?" Duke raises an eyebrow, clearly intrigued.

"I'm guessing they're all clues to where we're going," I speculate.

"They are," he confirms with a smile playing on his lips.

"Can I have any more clues?" I ask, eager for more hints.

"Okay, just one. The date is from a book. A book that was eventually turned into a movie," Duke reveals.

"That narrows it down," I chuckle, shaking my head at the challenge. Realizing I'm not going to get anywhere with that line of questioning, I decide to change the subject. "Where did you live before Washington?"

"New York City," Duke replies simply.

I've never been there, but everyone knows about New York. It's the city that doesn't sleep. I used to want to go there, to experience what life would be like in such an exciting place. But I've been careful to put those thoughts to rest. Afraid that if I went and liked it, that same restlessness that caused my mother to walk out on us would settle in me. But why would someone who lived in a city that looks as magical as New York want to leave and come to a small town in Georgia? "What made you want to come here?"

"Well, I'd never lived anywhere outside of Manhattan. Life in the city is exciting, but it's also nonstop. After a while, it becomes exhausting," he explains. "I was looking for something different—slower. That's when I saw Washington on TV."

"The Home Channel?" I inquire, curious about his reasons for moving.

"Yep. Nothing was keeping me in the city. So, I packed my things and moved," Duke confirms, his tone casual.

"Don't you have family in New York?" I ask, wondering about his ties to the city.

"My parents retired a few years back and moved to the suburbs in New Jersey," he explains, turning on the blinker. "They're only a plane ride away."

Duke turns off the main road, and we pass a large sign for Elijah Clark State Park. A few minutes later, the sparkling lake comes into view. Several boats are on the water enjoying the warm early December day.

"We're having a picnic at the lake?" I smile proudly, feeling accomplished for figuring out part of the date. However, I'm still unsure about the book reference.

"You're getting warmer," Duke confirms, offering a hint with a cryptic smile.

Duke pulls the car into a parking spot. Like a perfect gentleman, he opens my door and offers his hand to help me out. Then, he grabs the picnic basket from the backseat.

Looking around, it's clear we're nowhere near the picnic areas. I'm just about to tell him I think we parked in the wrong lot, but he beats me to it.

"We're going this way," he says, taking my hand and leading me toward the boat rental stand. After giving his name, we're escorted to a waiting rowboat.

"Can you hold this while I get in?" he asks, passing the picnic basket to me.

"Sure," I reply, taking the basket from him and eagerly anticipating our adventure.

The clerk holds the boat steady while Duke steps off the dock. Once he's situated, I pass the picnic basket to him. He sets it aside and offers me his hand. Carefully, I step off the dock. But my efforts at caution are for naught. My shoelace catches on a loose board, catapulting my body off the dock. Duke does his best to catch me, but it's no use. He lands on the bottom of the boat with me on top of him. I watch in horror as my little red sneaker flies over our heads and plops into the water.

"Are you okay?" Duke grabs my shoulders.

"I'm fine." Beyond humiliated, but unhurt. "I'm more worried about you."

"I'm good." He steadies me while I crawl off him and find my footing. Then, he climbs to his feet.

The dock attendant is staring at me, doing his best to suppress a laugh. "You both good?"

"We are. Can you untie us so we can retrieve her shoe?"

I look over Duke's shoulder and see my shoe bobbing away from us.

The kid works quickly, releasing the boat. Duke grabs the oars and begins rowing with ease. As he strokes, I stare at the well-defined muscles in his arms that stretch the T-shirt he's wearing. It's clear he works out. And I can't lie, I'm very much enjoying the view. It's taking my mind off the catastrophe that just ensued.

When we get close to my floating shoe, Duke reaches over the edge of the boat. "Got it." He holds up my sneaker as water pours out of it. "I don't think you're going to be wearing it anytime soon, though."

"Thanks." I take the soaking wet sneaker and remove the piece of seaweed stuck to it, dropping it back into the water. I slip off my other shoe and set them aside, thankful I stayed up late to paint my toenails. "You've done this before?" I motion to his capable rowing skills.

"I was on the rowing team at Columbia," Duke mentions casually.

"I'm impressed," I respond, genuinely impressed by his athleticism.

"It was nothing, really," he shrugs, downplaying his achievement. "We're going to head over this way. I'm told there have been sightings of Bald Eagles."

"*The Notebook*," I exclaim suddenly, recognizing the reference.

"Dumb idea, huh?" Duke asks, seeming uncertain.

"Not at all. It's one of my favorite books. And I've never seen an Eagle," I assure him.

"Outside of a zoo, neither have I," Duke admits.

"Are you hungry?" I inquire.

"I am," he confirms, pausing in his rowing. "This should be a good spot."

I open the picnic basket and start taking the food out. Duke thought ahead and had the sandwiches and salads pre-packaged in serving-sized containers so we wouldn't have to attempt to make plates on a boat.

"So, have you always lived in Washington?" Duke inquires about my background.

"I have," I reply.

"Did you ever want to leave?"

That question brings up painful memories of my mom. She was raised in Washington but traveled with her parents—she saw so much of the world. When I was a little girl, she'd pull out her photo albums and tell me stories about all the places she visited. I was enthralled by her tales and wanted to see all the places she told me about for myself.

But then she left.

"When I was young, sure. After my mom left, I blamed all the big cities for taking her away," I explain, reminiscing about my past. "Ridiculous, I know. But the young me had to direct her anger somewhere, I guess."

"I had no idea," Duke responds, sounding sympathetic.

"I've gotten over my anger since then," I assure him.

"How old were you?" he asks gently.

"Ten," I reply, feeling a pang of sadness at the memory.

"Do you ever hear from her? You don't have to answer that," Duke adds, sensing the sensitivity of the topic.

"It's okay. She left and never looked back. I have no idea where she is or if she's even alive," I reveal, my voice tinged with resignation.

"I'm sorry, Percy," Duke offers his condolences.

I go to speak, but movement in the sky over Duke's head catches my attention. "Look," I exclaim, pointing up. "It's a Bald Eagle."

With its wings outstretched, it looks completely effortless for the majestic bird to soar across the sky. As if in reverence of the eagle's appearance, the world around us is silent. The beauty of the moment brings tears to my eyes.

"Are you okay?" Duke asks, placing his hand over mine, concerned.

"It's incredible," I say in awe, my gaze fixed on the majestic bird.

We watch until the bird disappears into the tall trees surrounding the lake.

"Wow. That was amazing," Duke remarks, breaking the silence.

"It was. I can't thank you enough, Duke. I'll never forget this experience," I express my gratitude sincerely.

"I was afraid you were going to think my date idea was stupid," Duke admits, sounding relieved.

"You put a lot of planning into this. Of course, I'd love it," I reassure him, smiling warmly.

We float around on the lake while we talk. Conversation is surprisingly easy, and I find that although we grew up worlds apart, we have so much in common. The breeze begins to cool as the sun travels across the lake and begins to set.

"We should probably start heading back." Duke picks up the oars.

"We should probably start heading back," Duke suggests, picking up the oars to begin rowing.

"Can I try?" I inquire eagerly.

"Sure," Duke agrees, handing me the oars with a smile.

I'm shocked at how heavy the old wooden oars are by themselves, but when I lower them into the water, they're nearly impossible for me to lift. My arms try to pull back at the same time—like Duke showed me, but I don't have the upper body strength needed to pull them out of the water.

The left oar begins to slip from my grasp. In a futile attempt to save it, I drop the other one. Both of my hands grab the left oar, and it pops out, dousing us both with the cool lake water.

"Oh no," I shout and shift quickly, trying to save the right oar from falling off the boat and into the water. My jerky movements nearly capsize our small vessel.

"It's okay, Percy," Duke says, laughing, and points to a mechanism on the side of the boat. "They won't go anywhere, and even if they did, they'd float."

"I wish I had known that a few minutes ago," I say as I wipe my wet hair from my face. "I think maybe you should take over."

Duke and I switch spots as he takes the reigns once again. Having tried my hand at rowing, I have an even better appreciation for Duke's strength and ability to make the task look so easy.

I waited nearly thirty years for my first date, and it was beyond my expectations. From the start, with all those silly little poems that sent me on a scavenger hunt all around town, Duke went out of his way to make sure today was special. I hope my clumsiness didn't ruin it for him.

We arrive back at my house, and he walks me to my door.

"Thank you for everything. I had the best day ever," I express gratefully.

"I'm glad. So did I," Duke responds, smiling warmly. "I'd like to do it again."

"Me too. How about tomorrow?" I suggest, feeling a surge of boldness.

Tomorrow? Seriously, Percy? Desperate much?

"I'd like that," Duke agrees, surprising me with his lack of hesitation.

"Oh," I say, taken aback by his response. "How about you come over, and I'll cook dinner? Maybe we can watch a movie or something?"

"That sounds perfect," Duke replies, his smile widening.

Then, he does something even more shocking. Duke leans in, and his lips meet mine. It's a gentle, sweet kiss—my first kiss.

"Goodnight, Percy. I'll see you tomorrow," Duke says softly before turning to leave, leaving me in a daze.

Stunned from the kiss, I'm rendered speechless, unable to even manage a goodbye.

Duke

As I step back, I notice the shocked expression on Percy's face. I hadn't intended to kiss her—it just happened. She doesn't even say goodbye to me. I'm confident that by the time I get home, I'll have a text telling me to forget our date tomorrow.

The entire drive back to my house is spent mentally chastising myself for messing up the best day of my life. Once I'm home, I use the app to let the rental company know the car's ready to be picked up.

I'm microwaving myself some dinner when the phone buzzes. There's the text I was waiting for. Part of me wants to ignore it, to remain oblivious about my mistake for a while longer. But then I figure, why prolong the inevitable, so I pick up my cell to check the message.

Percy:

> Thank you again. I had a wonderful time to-day. If it's okay with you, we can walk to my house together after work for dinner.

Realizing she's not canceling on me, I quickly send her a text in response.

Duke:

> I had a great time, too. And that sounds per-fect.

Duke:

> I thought for sure you were going to cancel tomorrow.

Percy:

> Cancel? Why would I do that?

Duke:

> The kiss. I overstepped. I apologize.

Percy:

> It was perfect. Can I tell you something without you laughing at me?

Duke:

> Of course.

Percy:

> That was my first kiss.

The expression on her face suddenly makes sense. She wasn't upset. It was simply because she had never been kissed before.Top of Form

Duke:

> I'm honored.

Percy:

> Goodnight Duke.

Duke:

Sleep well.

I'm her first kiss. How could this intelligent, beautiful, and kind woman have never been kissed before?

I wouldn't say I have a lot of experience with girls, but I've dated some. My first kiss was with my high school girlfriend, Ruby Thatcher. We met during our junior year of high school. She'd just transferred schools and joined the math club. We hit it off immediately and started dating. Living in the city, we were never at a loss for something fun to do and often went to the museums on the weekend.

We got along well, and I thought we had a lot of fun. We dated throughout most of our senior year. The prom was in a few weeks. I'd just purchased our tickets and was going to ask her to be my date. I rounded the corner of our high school's hall and saw Andrew, president of the yearbook committee, leaning against her locker. Ruby dumped me later that afternoon. As for prom, I didn't go.

Then, during my first year at Columbia, I met Samantha Raven. She sat next to me in my Intro to Psychology course. She was originally from a small town in North Dakota. Samantha came to Columbia to study Drama and Theater arts. Samantha had stars in her eyes and dreamt of landing a leading role in a Broadway show. She was excited to be dating someone who was on the rowing team, and I was excited to have a pretty girl on my arm. It only took a few weeks for her to realize I wasn't the popular party guy she was looking for. It was a Friday night, and I was on my way to her dorm to pick her up when I got a text.

I did the walk of shame to the edge of campus, where I spotted Samantha on the arm of one of the football players. She didn't care that he had a reputation for dating a different girl every week, just that he was popular. And that his father was in the carpenter's union and built sets for Broadway shows.

Clearly, my judgment of the opposite sex wasn't the best.

That was the last time I took a chance on a girl until Percy. I'm not shy when it comes to girls. I just wasn't interested in getting hurt again. I was certain once she found out who was behind her scavenger hunt, she'd laugh in my face and turn me down. Instead, she surprised me and said yes. And even better than that, we had a terrific day together.

Monday morning rolls around again. Instead of dreading getting out of bed to start yet another work week, I'm up before my alarm and ready to start my day. I even thought ahead. Before I went to bed last night, I laid my clothes out. Khaki pants and an emerald polo shirt. I didn't want anything to keep me from getting into town early today. Then, I grab my messenger bag and head out the door.

"Good morning, Harold," I greet before the driver has a chance to welcome me.

"You're mighty happy this morning," Harold remarks, glancing at me through the rearview mirror.

"Life is good," I reply with a smile, reaching forward to clasp his shoulder before taking my seat behind him.

"You've either won the lottery or met a girl," Harold observes with a chuckle.

"Not just any girl. *The girl*," I clarify, feeling a surge of excitement.

"Ah. Young love," Harold chuckles again, closing the doors and starting the drive.

Percy

"He kissed me," I squeal as soon as Aurora answers the call.

"Oh, Perc. I'm so happy for you. Tell me everything," Aurora responds eagerly, her voice filled with excitement.

I sink into the buttery soft leather of my sofa and recount all the details of the special day Duke and I shared—minus the mishaps. "I couldn't have imagined a better first date. And he's coming over for dinner after work tomorrow," I conclude with a satisfied sigh.

"I knew you two would be perfect together," Aurora remarks, her voice brimming with joy.

"You were right," I admit with a chuckle.

"Can you say that again?" she teases, laughing.

"You were right," I repeat, rolling my eyes playfully. "See you tomorrow."

Knowing I always run late, I choose my outfit for tomorrow and then crawl into bed. The cats take their usual spots, and I drift off to sleep and dream about the handsome man I'm quickly falling for.

I set my alarm twenty minutes early as another precaution against being late. It's an absolutely beautiful Monday morning. There's still a little chill in the air, so I throw on a sweater before taking the cats for their morning walk. If my neighbors thought I was crazy walking two cats, I've left no doubt in their minds now that I'm walking three. It doesn't bother us, though. I enjoy the fresh air, and the cats seem to love getting out to explore.

After our walk, I feed the cats and sit down with a bowl of oatmeal and blueberries. Then, after a quick shower, I do my hair and get dressed.

It's the first full week in December, which means Christmas is just a few weeks away. The holiday season is hands down my favorite time of the year. I've amassed a wardrobe specifically for the countdown to Christmas. Today, I'm wearing a vintage-style dark green dress with a sweetheart neckline. The skirt has a cute peek-a-boo layer made of red plaid that matches the bow on the front. I've paired it with black-heeled Mary Jane's, my go-to style of choice, with a sparkly picture of Santa's face on the front.

I'm ready nearly twenty minutes ahead of schedule, something practically unheard of for me. With my bag in hand, I say goodbye to the cats and head off to Duke—I mean work.

His One, Her Only Publishing

To: M. Loveless

I'm pleased to tell you everything is all set with Janelle Graham. The Washington, Georgia Nooks with Books store has agreed to host Resolution: Romance. An evening with M. Loveless. She's also in possession of the promotional materials and is handling all the details on their end.

She'll be reaching out to the store manager, Ms. Persephone Douglas, this week to inform her of the event and coordinate everything on the local level.

I'll be flying into town for the event as well. Do you have any suggestions on accommodations in the Washington area?

I look forward to meeting you in person.

Warmest Regards,

Madeliene Bennet

Publicity Executive

M. Loveless

To: Madeline Bennet

Thank you for the update on the event. I'm familiar with Ms. Graham and am confident everything's in capable hands.

I would suggest staying at The Fitzpatrick Hotel. It's a historic building dating back to 1898 and is located right on the Town Square. I'm sure you will find the accommodations more than suitable for your stay.

I look forward to meeting you as well.

Sincerely,

M. Loveless

Percy

As I'm about to grasp the café door handle, Duke rushes over to me.

"Allow me," Duke says, pulling the door open.

"Thank you," I reply with a smile.

"Morning sunshine," Chris says, surprising me with his presence.

"You're home!" I exclaim, rushing over to him and being swept off my feet. "I'm so glad to see you."

"Me too," Chris responds, planting a kiss on my cheek.

I glance over my shoulder at Duke, who's shooting daggers in Chris's direction.

"Duke, I'd like to introduce Chris, Aurora's boyfriend," I say, gesturing towards Chris.

"Nice to meet you," Duke replies, visibly relaxing as he steps forward to shake Chris's outstretched hand.

"Make that fiancée," Aurora announces as she exits the kitchen.

"Fiancée?" I echo in surprise.

Aurora holds up her left hand, showing off the shimmering diamond engagement ring on her finger.

"You didn't tell me you got engaged," I remark, surprised.

"I wasn't engaged until this morning," Aurora explains, sidling up to Chris, who puts his arm around her.

"I'm so happy for you both. When's the wedding?" I inquire eagerly.

"We're looking at an early spring date," Chris answers. "We've been together long enough that we don't need a lengthy engagement."

"I can't believe it. Can you?" I turn to Duke.

"Me? Nope, can't believe it," Duke responds with a grin.

Aurora brings fresh muffins to the table while I carry the drinks. Then, the four of us sit down for breakfast. While we eat, the happy couple tells us all their plans for their wedding.

"You'll be my maid of honor, right?" Aurora asks with a hopeful smile.

"Of course," I reply, wiping a stray tear that drips down my cheek. "I can't believe my bestie's getting married."

"Neither can I," Aurora admits, sharing in my disbelief.

Aurora and I look at pictures of wedding dresses and flowers. The guys, who seem to have hit it off right away, have their heads together going over the website Duke built for Muffins and Meows.

I'm so caught up in the moment I realize I forgot to keep an eye on the time. When I glance at my phone, I panic. "I was supposed to open the store five minutes ago." I jump from my seat and scramble to clean up my dishes.

"Don't worry about those. I'll get them," Aurora says, waving me off.

"Thanks," I reply gratefully.

"I'll be over in a few minutes," Duke chimes in, looking up from the laptop.

"Okay. See you soon," I respond, smiling at him.

I fumble through my bag, looking for the keys as I rush next door. To my relief, Houston's early and has the store open.

"I'm sorry I'm late," I apologize, slightly out of breath.

"Not a problem," Houston reassures me as he sets up for the children, who should start showing up any minute for storytime.

"I have to run back and check my emails. I'll take story time today," I declare.

"Are you sure?" Houston asks, sounding concerned.

"Yep," I confirm with a nod, determined to fulfill my responsibilities.

I hurry to the back and log into my email. There are always messages from the home office about one thing or another. Most of the emails are the standard ones I expect to find on a Monday morning, that is, until I come to the last one. My mouth hangs open as I read it.

To: **Persephone Douglas**
From: **Janelle Graham**

Persephone,

I have very exciting news to share with you. Last week, I received a phone call from Madeleine Bennet, a publicity executive at His One, Her Only Publishing. She informed me that M. Loveless has agreed to have a coming-out party of sorts. Even more exciting is the news that the author personally requested our Washington, Georgia, store. The event, Resolution: Romance. An evening with M. Loveless will be held on New Year's Eve.

I asked Ms. Bennet why the Washington, Georgia store as opposed to our flagship store in Manhattan. What she said next shocked me, and I'm sure will do the same to you. Apparently, M. Loveless lives in Washington. What are the chances of that? This is not only a huge opportunity for Nooks with Books but also for your store.

I want to speak to you about making this event something unique to Washington. Can you do a virtual meeting with me at about three p.m.?

I look forward to speaking to you this afternoon.

Janelle Graham

District Manager, Nooks with Books

I drop my head into my hands, trying to let that email sink in. In only three weeks, everyone will know who M. Loveless is. Nothing will ever be the same. I'm still trying to process everything when I hear a knock on the door.

"Come in," I beckon.

"Is everything okay?" Houston asks with concern.

"No," I reply, motioning for him to come closer. "Read this."

Houston takes a few moments to read the email. "Wow. M. Loveless lives in Washington and is going to do their first signing at our store?"

"It appears that way," I confirm, feeling a bit overwhelmed.

"That's incredible," Houston remarks, his excitement palpable.

"Sure," I respond nonchalantly, unable to muster the same enthusiasm.

"Why aren't you more excited about this? It's huge," Houston presses, noticing my lack of enthusiasm.

I let out a big sigh. "Maybe they just wanted to live their unassuming life without anyone learning who they are. Instead, they're being forced to do a signing and reveal their identity."

"How do you know they're being forced to do this?" Houston raises an eyebrow.

"I don't know for sure," I hastily reply, hitting the reply button. "It's just a guess."

"Mhm," Houston murmurs thoughtfully.

"What's that supposed to mean?" I inquire, feeling a bit defensive.

"I know you moonlight as a romance author," Houston reveals, his smirk evident.

"Me?" I feign surprise.

"Yes, you," Houston confirms. "And I think this proves it."

I can't help but laugh. "You're hilarious. Did you need something?"

"Oh yeah. The kids are here," Houston reminds me.

"I have to send a quick reply to Janelle, and then I'll be out," I inform him.

"I'll sing 'Jingle Bells' to keep them busy, M. Loveless," he jests, walking out of the office and leaving me shaking my head in amusement.

Quickly, I type an email to Janelle letting her know I'll be able to do a video call this afternoon. Then, with another deep breath, I make my way out to the waiting children.

Duke

"The site looks great," Chris compliments.

"When will it be live?" he inquires.

"I'm planning on putting the finishing elements in today. Is it okay if I show them to you tomorrow?" I ask Aurora. "I have a prior engagement after work."

"By prior engagement, he means a date with Percy," Aurora interjects, playfully waggling her eyebrows.

"You and Percy are dating?" Chris asks, surprised.

"I don't know if we're dating, exactly. But I am going to her house for dinner," I explain.

"And they were out together yesterday," Aurora adds, further elaborating.

"Sounds like you're dating to me," Chris remarks, sitting back and crossing his arms. "What are your intentions with Percy?"

"My intentions?" I repeat, caught off guard.

"Yes," Chris says with a serious expression.

"Well, I hadn't really thought about it—" I begin, uncertainly.

"You're terrible, Chris," Aurora elbows him. "Ignore him," she advises, starting to clear the table.

"Be kind to her. She's like a sister to me, and I don't want to see her get hurt," Chris advises me solemnly.

"Will do," I assure him, closing my laptop and sliding it into my bag. "I need to get going. I have a lot to accomplish today."

"See you later," Aurora calls from the kitchen.

"It was nice to meet you," I say to Chris on my way out.

When I get into the bookstore, I look around for Percy, but I don't see her anywhere. Come to think of it, I don't see Houston either. What I do see is a group of young children getting their mats ready for storytime.

I take my seat and pull my laptop out. While I'm waiting for it to turn on, Houston comes from the back hall wearing a huge grin on his face and singing 'Jingle Bells.' By the time he gets to the chorus, the group of little voices has joined him, singing the familiar Christmas song.

A few minutes later, Percy steps out from the back. Instead of a smile, she's as white as a ghost. She meets my stare and manages a small, unsure smile before she takes over for Houston. After one more song, she gets the children settled on their mats and begins reading *How the Grinch Stole Christmas*. It's a story I've heard a million times, but I find myself enraptured as I listen to her retelling of the tale.

As much as I'd love to sit here and watch Percy all afternoon, I have projects that need to be completed. Somehow, I manage to drag my attention away from her and back to my laptop. It takes a concerted effort to stay focused on my work.

It's another forty-five minutes before the kids, with their crafts in hand, exit the store. After Percy finishes cleaning up the area, she stops by my table on her way to the trash can.

"Is everything okay?" I ask, noticing Percy's troubled expression as she emerges from her office.

"What do you mean?" she responds, attempting to brush off her concerns.

"When you came out of your office, you looked like something was wrong," I observe, sensing her unease.

She throws away the remnants of craft and snack time before sitting down, clearly conflicted. "I had an email from my boss about an upcoming event." I raise an eyebrow, intrigued. "There's a romance author set to come here in a few weeks."

"You've had author events here before. They aren't that bad, are they?" I probe.

"Ordinarily, no. But this one's a really big deal," she admits, her tone heavy with concern.

"Oh?" I prompt, sensing there's more to the story.

She sighs. "The identity of the author is a mystery."

"Is it that M something or another person?" I ask, recalling the mysterious author whose books dominate our display.

"You know who M. Loveless is?" She looks genuinely surprised.

"I sit in a bookstore every day," I point out, gesturing toward the nearby display. "And this M. Loveless character has a huge display right there. Women are always over here talking about the mystery surrounding the author's identity."

"Right," she acknowledges, nodding slowly.

"It's amazing they're having an event like this in such a small store. I wonder why," I mull over the implications.

"Apparently, M. Loveless lives in Washington," she explains, resting her chin in her hands. "I'm just not looking forward to this at all."

"But you love romance books," I remind her.

"I do. I just think their identity should remain a secret. That's part of what's so special about them," Percy confesses, her expression conflicted. "I have to get back to work. Houston needs to take his break."

With less enthusiasm than I've ever seen from her, Percy gets up and walks over to the register. I'm left to wonder why she's so disappointed at the thought of discovering who this mystery author really is.

Percy

THE AFTERNOON SHOPPERS HAVE cleared out. Houston should be able to handle the floor with no problems while I'm in the office on the video conference. I click the link and wait to be let into the virtual meeting room. It's only a minute before a box pops up, and I see Janelle.

"Hi, Percy. How's everything going?" Janelle's voice cuts through the quiet of the bookstore.

"Everything's well," I reply with a faint smile.

"What did you think about that email? It's super exciting, isn't it?" Janelle's enthusiasm is palpable.

"It's unbelievable," I manage, trying to match her energy.

"Since it's going to be New Year's Eve, I'm thinking we can make it more than a simple book signing. I'm picturing a full-on party to ring in the New Year."

"Oh," I respond, caught off guard by the unexpected suggestion. "I'd like to feature businesses from Washington for the event. Nothing extravagant," she explains thoughtfully. "I'm thinking some finger foods, desserts, and flowers. Things like that. Would you be able to recommend some places?"

"Sure. I know the perfect places," I offer, feeling a glimmer of excitement. One of them is Muffins and Meows. This could be a huge break for Aurora.

"Great. Can you email me their contact information, and I'll contact them?" "I can. Is there anything else?" I inquire, eager to assist in any way I can.

"Corporate will be sending new displays for the store in about two weeks. Oh, and you'll receive a package with the decorations for the night of the party. I know it's only the two of you. Will you be able to handle getting the store ready yourselves, or should I look into hiring a decorator?"

"I have some friends I can ask to pitch in if that's okay," I suggest, feeling relieved to have a solution.

"That's perfect," Janelle responds with a satisfied nod.□

"While we're talking. Did you receive my request to hire one or two part-timers?" Janelle's voice holds a hint of anticipation.

"I did. I had to get approval from the home office, which just came through yesterday. I want to offer Houston an assistant man-ager position," I reply, feeling a sense of relief.

"That's wonderful," she responds with a smile in her voice. "It'll bump his hours up to full-time, which will alleviate some of the extra hours you put in every week. And I also have permission to hire four part-time staff."

"Terrific. I appreciate that," I say, genuinely grateful.

"Please keep this between us for now," Janelle adds, sounding cautious. "I will," I assure her. "Is there anything else?" she asks, wrapping up the conversation.

"I don't think so," I respond, feeling satisfied.

"Great. I'll give you a call to check on everything right before Christmas. If anything comes up in the meantime, you have my cell," she concludes, her tone reassuring.

We say our goodbyes, and the screen goes black. Then, I drop my head into my hands. I'm sure readers will think this is the event of the year, but I'm absolutely dreading it.

Duke accompanies me on the walk home from work. Our dinner date is tonight, and as excited as I am, I also feel like a grey cloud has been hanging over me since the M. Loveless news.

"You seem a million miles away," Duke observes as we stroll down the sidewalk.

"Me?" I glance at him, surprised by his insight.

"Are you okay?" He looks genuinely concerned.

"I guess so," I reply, trying to sound more convincing than I feel.

"Would you rather cancel tonight?" he asks, his voice soft with understanding.

"What?" I stop walking, taken aback. "No. Why would you think that?"

"You haven't said two words since we left the store," he points out gently.

"I'm sorry. It's this M. Loveless event. I'm not thrilled about it," I admit, feeling the weight of my concerns.

"You mentioned that. Is there anything I can do to help?" Duke offers, his tone reassuring.

"Do you like planning events?" I ask, a glimmer of hope in my voice.

"I've never done it. But I'm willing to learn," he replies with a reassuring smile.

When we get into the house, we're immediately greeted by a furry welcoming party.

"Hey there." I stoop down to pet the cats. "Did you miss me?"

Each of them fights for my attention, that is, until Tess notices Duke. I may as well be chopped liver or a pate, perhaps, because suddenly my pets aren't acceptable. She goes right to Duke, who bends down and lifts her into his arms.

"Hi, girl. How are you today?" Duke greets Tess with a head butt from the affectionate cat.

"So much for loyalty to the person who feeds you," I tease, slipping off my shoes. "You can leave your bag here." I gesture to the bench. "Or in the library if you prefer."

"Thanks," Duke acknowledges, leaving his bag on a chair in the library. With Tess still in his arms, he follows me into the kitchen.

"Can I get you something to drink?" I inquire.

"I'll have some water," he replies.

I fetch a glass of ice water for him. "Make yourself at home. I have to go upstairs and take care of a few cat chores, then I'll get dinner started."

Duke gently sets Tess down. "How about I take care of the cats?"

"You don't have to do that," I protest.

"I'm offering," he insists.

"If you say so," I acquiesce with a shrug.

I can't help but smile, watching Duke walk toward the steps with Tess glued to his side. Everyone always says pets are a good gauge of a person's character. It's clear Duke's passed the test there.

Once he's out of sight. I pull out the tofu I've had marinating in a jerk seasoning, plantains, cabbage, and several other ingredients and get started preparing our dinner.

Duke

I MAKE MY WAY upstairs with Percy's tiger cat, my new best friend, at my side. When I get to the cat's room, I find the other two felines hanging out in front of the window.

I spot the litter box in the corner. It's one of those fancy self-cleaning ones, so emptying it's a breeze. There's a water bowl up here as well, so I make sure to give them fresh water from the bathroom sink. Then, I make my way back to the staircase. Except, I get distracted along the way.

From the loft, I can see Percy in the kitchen. She has music playing as she chops vegetables for whatever dish she's making. While I'm watching, Tess jumps on the desk where Percy's laptop is. She bats a pen off the desk, and I pick it up. When I go to put it back on the desk, Tess walks over to the laptop's keyboard, and the screen comes to life. "Come on, girl. Let's get down before you mess up whatever your mommy's working on." I carefully shoo the cat off the desk, intending to close the laptop, but I get sidetracked when I look at the screen. Percy's a writer. Not just any writer, but a romance writer. Without conscious thought, I sit in the chair and start reading her work. She's really good.

"What are you doing?" Percy's voice startles me.

I jump from the seat. "It's not what it looks like."

"It isn't?" She crosses her arms, skeptical.

"Well, it is. But it's not why you're thinking." She stares at me but doesn't say anything. "Tess jumped on the keyboard. I got her off and was going to close the computer so you didn't lose whatever you were working on. But I read the first line and got sucked into your story." I take a breath. "You're a very good writer. Have you ever published your writing?"

"Thank you. And yes, I have." She closes her laptop. "But my writing is something most people don't know about, and I'd like to keep it that way."

"I'm sorry. I shouldn't have invaded your privacy like that."

"It's fine. I just don't like to make a big deal about it."

"I'll forget I ever saw it."

A smile graces her lips.

While Percy puts the finishing touches on the meal, I set the table. I've never done something so domestic with a woman before. It's a comfortable feeling, one I decide is something I can get used to. I wonder if Percy feels the same way, but I don't want to ask. I don't want to scare her with these crazy thoughts I'm having. I'm setting our glasses on the table when Percy comes over with two bowls of something that looks amazing and smells even better.

"What is it?"

"It's a jerk tofu grain bowl. I hope you like it."

When Percy asked about my food preferences, I told her to make whatever she was making for herself. She reminded me she's vegan and offered to cook meat for me. Even though I was slightly apprehensive about what a vegan meal would taste like, I declined the meat option. Now, I'm glad I did.

We sit down together, and I grab the fork to take my first bite. Percy watches me closely. I try to school my features as I chew my food.

"What's the verdict?" she asks hesitantly.

"It's delicious." The vegetables provide the dish with vibrant color and fresh flavor. The marinated tofu gives it a spicy kick. "I love it."

She lets out a breath and smiles. "I was worried you wouldn't like it."

"I was a bit nervous, too," I admit. "But if this is what vegan meals are like, I don't think I'd miss eating meat."

"I've gotten much better over the years."

Percy tells me more about how she learned to cook after her mom left. Knowing the circumstances, I find myself surprised at how much she's grown to love the task.

"I envy your ability to cook. My mom never let me in the kitchen, so I exist on microwave meals," I confess.

"I always make extra. I'd be happy to share with you," she offers.

"You don't have to do that," I reply.

"I know, but I'd like to," she insists.

"How can I argue with a pretty girl?" I tease.

"You can't," she giggles.

"Thank you. I really appreciate it," I express my gratitude. Eating processed microwave foods gets old quickly.□

When we've finished the meal, Percy packages some leftovers for her lunch tomorrow and a take-home container for me. Then, just like on Thanksgiving, we do the dishes together.

"How old were you when you stopped believing in the tooth fairy?" she asks.

"Someone was on Real Life Romance again." I smile.

"Maybe," she replies with a shrug.

"Who says I stopped believing? What about you?" I counter."

I was about seven, I think," she begins, wiping her hands on the dishtowel before leaning against the counter to share her story. "It had been a long time since I lost a tooth. Looking back, I realized Mom was pretty much checked out at that point, so Dad was picking up all the slack. I put my tooth under my pillow but was disappointed when I found it still there in the morning. Later that evening, when Dad got home from work, I asked him if the tooth fairy ever forgot to visit a kid who had lost a tooth. He told me, of course not. When I showed him my tooth, Dad nearly broke down. He promised if I put it under my pillow again that night, the tooth fairy would come. After that conversation, I realized the tooth fairy wasn't real, but I didn't have the heart to tell Dad," she finishes with a wistful smile.

The sorrow reflected in her eyes pierces me. It stirs an impulse to envelop her in my arms and vow to shield her from any further pain.

Percy

"I'm sorry," I say, my voice softening.

"For what?" Duke turns to face me.

"I didn't mean to bring up sad memories."

"You asked the question, remember?" Unfortunately, my past is full of sad memories. Don't get me wrong, there are plenty of wonderful memories too. Still, for some reason, the good times often become overshadowed by the bad ones. "Would you like to watch a movie?"

"I'd love to." His eyes brighten with anticipation.

I make some popcorn and hot cocoa, then we make our way to the sofa. We decide on a Christmas movie about a nanny who falls in love with a handsome prince.□

Holiday movies are my favorite. They're some of the only stories where unlikely couples come together and find true love. If only real life was like that. I glance at the man sitting next to me, sipping his hot cocoa. Could he be my happy ending?

Two hours later, the movie is wrapping up. The prince asks the former nanny to marry him. They kiss and get their happily ever after. I swipe at the tears that never fail to fall when I watch Christmas movies.

"Are you okay?" Duke asks, concern marring his face.

"I'm a sucker for a happy ending," I admit with a smile.

"I know what you mean." His smile matches mine, but then he glances at his watch. "It's getting pretty late. I really should be going."

Duke gathers his things, and I walk him to the door.

"Thank you for coming over. I had a really nice time."

"So did I." He slings his messenger bag across his chest before he moves closer, pressing his lips against mine.

The kiss is tender and full of emotion.

"I'd like to see you again. And again." Duke's voice is deep and sexy. "If that's okay with you."

"I'd like that very much."

"Perhaps I could see you so much that I could call you my girlfriend." He pulls me against him as his hazel eyes search my face.

"I guess that means I'd call you my boyfriend?" I ask flirtatiously.

"I think that's how this works." He smiles, his dimple making an appearance. "Is that a yes?"

"That's a yes."

I barely finish speaking before he kisses me again. I don't have much experience in this area, but wow, can this guy kiss. Who would've known behind the shy computer guy that sits in my bookstore every day is this sweet and sexy man? And how did I get lucky enough that he asked me to be his girlfriend?

"Goodnight, Percy," he says quietly before turning and walking out the door.

I'm running later than usual this morning. My alarm was set early, but it went off right in the middle of a wonderful dream. Not wanting the dream to end, I thought I snoozed the alarm, but I must've turned it off instead. Luckily for me, Caspian woke me nearly a half hour after I should've been up.

I shoot out of bed in a panic and rush to shower and get dressed. On my way downstairs, my foot hits a cat toy, a ball, to be precise. It rolls over the top, and my body begins to fall. I grab the handrail, which is thankfully very secure in the wall. My heart is pounding as I regain my footing. I toss the ball back upstairs.

"I wish you cats could learn how to put your toys away," I yell, earning me a reproaching glare from the girls who are sitting at the bottom of the steps, flicking their tails and waiting for their breakfast.

After I get the cats set for the day, I grab my lunch bag out of the fridge and send a quick text to Houston.

Percy:

I overslept. I'm leaving now. I'll be there as fast as I can.

Houston:

Take your time. I've got it under control.

Percy:

> **You're a lifesaver.**

Typically, I'd wear heels to work, but today, I opt for my red sequin chucks. I'm in a hurry, and as comfortable as my Mary Jane's are, there's no way I could walk fast enough in them to get to work at any reasonable time.

While I'm tying the laces, the three cats weave their way around my feet. "Sorry, guys. We're going to have to skip our walk today." I feel bad interrupting our routine and disappointing them, but I have no choice. "I promise I'll get up early tomorrow." I give each one quick scratches behind their ears and then head out the door.

I've barely made it off my porch when my phone dings.

Duke:

> **You aren't here. Is everything okay?**

Percy:

> **I overslept. I'm on my way.**

I slide my phone into my pocket and start speed walking to work. I'm a bit out of breath when I get to the store.

"I'm so sorry, Houston," I apologize.

"It's really no big deal," he reassures me.

"Let me go put this stuff in the back, and I'll be right out." I gesture towards a pile of boxes on the floor behind the counter. "What's all that?"

"Not sure. They're addressed to you, so I didn't open them," he responds.

I quickly scan the store to ensure there's no one else around. "Do you mind opening them for me?" I ask.

"No problem," he agrees.

When I get to my office, I notice a bag from the café and a Banana Bubble Tea. There's a note next to them.

Percy,

I didn't want you to be hungry, so I grabbed you some breakfast.

Duke

Opening the bag, I find a Triple Berry Muffin. I sit down and take a bite.

Percy:

Thank you for breakfast. It was very thoughtful.

Duke:

I didn't want my girl to go hungry.

Percy:

I owe you another dinner.

Duke:

I won't turn that offer down.

His comment makes me laugh. I wish we could keep texting, but work calls. I open my email program to send an email to Janelle.

To: **Janelle Graham**

From: **Persephone Douglas**

Janelle,

I have a list of the businesses I think will be perfect for the New Year's Eve event. The Hot Box will be the ideal place to provide the food. Muffins and Meows café makes the best desserts around and is located right next door. The café also has an extensive list of coffees and teas. Hendrick's Florist does beautiful displays, and I'm confident will be able to handle whatever you're thinking about.

I've attached everyone's contact information to the email. Let me know if there's anything else you need.

~Percy Douglas

After wiping the crumbs off my clothes, I head back to the register to see what's in all those boxes. My jaw drops when I see what Houston's unpacked.

"Home office is serious about this signing." He gestures toward the counter.

"I guess so," I say as I look through the decorations, flyers, posters, and so much more. "Looks like we have our work cut out for us."

Percy

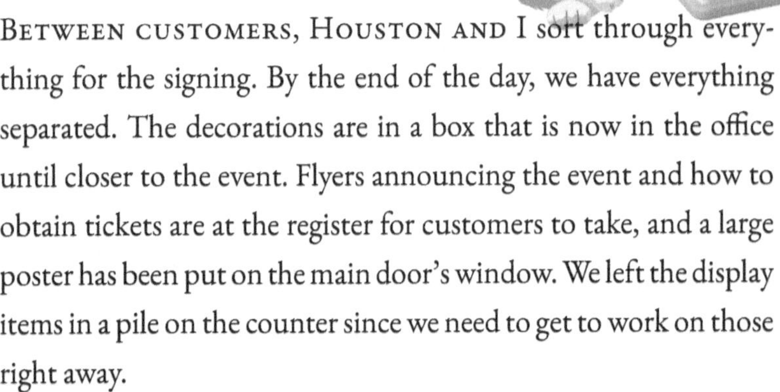

Between customers, Houston and I sort through everything for the signing. By the end of the day, we have everything
separated. The decorations are in a box that is now in the office
until closer to the event. Flyers announcing the event and how to
obtain tickets are at the register for customers to take, and a large
poster has been put on the main door's window. We left the display
items in a pile on the counter since we need to get to work on those
right away.

Houston locks up the store for the evening while I close the
register.

"We'll be closed on New Year's Eve so we can set up for the event.
Will you be able to come in to help?" I inquire.

"I wouldn't leave you hanging with this," Houston assures,
glancing around the store.

"Do you think the two of us are going to be able to get it all
done?"

"I'm going to ask Aurora and Chris to help," I reply.

"What about me?" Duke's sudden question startles me.

"I have your name down already," I respond with a smile. "I
think between the five of us, we should be okay. Before I go home,

I need to tell Aurora I volunteered her to cater the desserts for the event."

"I'm heading that way, too. May I walk with you?" he offers.

"I'd love that," I accept with a smile.

"M. Loveless is coming to your store?" Aurora squeals.

I roll my eyes. "Yes."

"How are you not crazy excited?"

"I'm thrilled, can't you tell? Anyway." I continue. "My district manager would like local businesses to provide food and drinks for the event. I hope you don't mind that I gave her your number."

"Of course, I don't mind."

"Excellent. Janelle will give you a call so you can discuss the contract and all that stuff." I wave my hand in the air.

"Thank you." She grabs me and squeezes tight. "I can't wait to tell Chris."

Duke gets a muffin to go, and we leave the café together. We're still outside talking when the bus pulls up.

"There's my ride. I'll see you tomorrow."

I watch as Duke begins to walk toward the bus.

"Wait," I call, and he turns around. "Why don't you come over for dinner again." It's less a question and more a statement. I hate the thought of him going home to a microwave meal.

"Are you sure? I don't want to impose."

"I'm positive."

Duke waves, letting the driver know he's not getting on. I get goosebumps as I watch him stride back toward me, his hazel eyes never breaking contact with mine. Duke takes my hand in his, a jolt of electricity shoots up my arm from the connection, and we begin the walk home.

Duke

WE GET TO HER house and do the same routine as yesterday, except this time, I don't invade her privacy on her laptop.

Tonight's dinner is handmade pasta and sauce.

"Doesn't pasta use eggs?" I inquire.

"Usually, but the recipe I use is eggless," Percy clarifies.

"What can I do to help?" I offer. "Do you mind opening the sauce and pouring it into the pot over there?" she requests.

"You can your own sauce?" I question, surprised.

"I do. My Nana taught me how to preserve food. We'd spend at least a full week every summer preserving vegetables and making sauce," she explains, a nostalgic smile playing on her lips.

"It helps me feel close to her still."

"That's a very special memory," I observe.

"It is," she agrees.□

We finish cooking dinner together. Percy patiently walks me through, heating up the sauce. I'm sure it's an easy task for most people, but it's a challenge for someone who can barely boil water.

"You haven't told me much about your family," she prompts as we settle down to eat. "What are your parents like?"

"Well, Mom's a retired pediatrician, and Dad's a retired attorney," I answer.

"Wow. That's impressive," she remarks.

"I guess. I just knew them as Mom and Dad," I shrug.

"Do you have siblings?" she inquires further.

"Nope. It's just me," I reply.

While we eat, I tell her about my old life in New York City. We compare our experiences, which couldn't have been more opposite if we'd tried.

Once we're done eating, I seize our empty dishes before Percy has a chance. "You get the night off," I insist.

"Duke," she protests.

"You cooked again. I'm doing the dishes."

"You helped."

"You did most of the work," I counter.

She reluctantly agrees, and while I load the dishwasher, Percy fills plastic containers with the leftovers.

"Tell me more about your family," she prompts.

"My parents and I have a good relationship. We keep in touch, especially since I've moved down here. We call each other almost every night."

"Are you going to see them for the holidays?" she inquires.

"Actually, I was thinking about inviting them here. There's a woman I'd like to introduce them to."

"You want me to meet your parents?"

"If that's okay with you. Unless you think it's too soon?"

"I'd love to meet them," she responds warmly, putting a pot in the sink and kissing my cheek. "Do you think they'll like me?"

"They're going to love you," I assure her, knowing that because I already do.

Percy

I'M SURE MY STOMACH has a permanent case of butterflies. Duke wants to introduce me to his parents. Even though he's reassured me they'll like me, I'm worried they'll find me completely inadequate to date their son.

"Do you have to leave right away?" I ask, a hopeful look in her eyes.

"Not unless you want me to," Duke replies.

"I was hoping maybe you'd help me decorate my Christmas tree."

"I'm afraid I might not be much good at it," Duke admits.

"Why not?" My curiosity piques.

"I'm embarrassed to say this, but I've never decorated a tree before."

"You do celebrate Christmas, right?"

"Yes. Growing up, my parents always hired a decorator for their house. When I moved out, I never bothered to decorate my place."

I try to hide the shock I experience when Duke tells me his parents used to hire a decorator. I've seen stuff like that on television, but I've never met anyone who could afford a luxury like that.

"Tonight's the perfect night for you to learn," I say with a grin.

While Duke carries the containers from the loft into the living room, I put Christmas music on. Then, I click the switch, lighting up the tree.

As I take out the carefully packed ornaments, I'm hit with the same onslaught of memories that awaits me every year. My Baby's First Christmas ornament is the first one out.

"Is there a story behind this?" Duke points at the crack down the center that my dad superglued.

"There is," I confirm, my voice soft with nostalgia.□

I was thirteen years old. We'd just finished decorating when our cat Gilbert decided to investigate the tree. Dad tried to stop him, but the cat was too fast. He leaped from the mantle above the fireplace three-quarters of the way up the tree. But he didn't quite make it. He tried to hold onto the edge of the branch, his back legs desperately kicking, attempting to grab something—anything. The tree wobbled back and forth. Gil got spooked and landed on the floor with a loud meow. He took off just as the tree toppled over. The tree and the ornaments hit the floor.

Dad got the tree back up and was inspecting the damage when I found my porcelain ornament lying in two pieces. I fell to my knees, sobbing. As usual, Dad came to the rescue. He held up the pieces, showing me how easily they'd come back together. I knelt on the chair next to Dad as he glued my precious ornament. Then, he wiped away my tears. Once the glue dried, he helped me hang it back onto the tree that had been tied to the wall with fishing line. I smile as I recall the memory.

"Your father sounds like he was a good man," Duke observes.

"He was the best. He's the standard I've always measured men by." I hang the ornament. "I guess that's part of the reason why I've never really dated."

"Never dated?" Duke's tone holds a hint of surprise.

Realizing my slip-up, I try to backtrack, but it's too late. The truth is out.

"Um. Yeah. I've never had a boyfriend."

Duke strides over to me, brushing a piece of hair behind my ear. His knuckles graze my cheek in the process. "How is it that a beautiful woman like you has never dated?"

"There was never anyone who interested me. Until you."

Duke

I can hardly believe my ears. Percy's never had a boyfriend. It's not that I've dated a ton, but I have dated. "I'm honored to be your first," I say with a smile.

"I'm glad it's you, too," she replies, wrapping her arms around my neck.

That knowledge does something to me, and I can't help but kiss this amazing woman I'm holding in my arms. "I hope to have many more firsts together," I whisper.

An hour later, we finish decorating the tree and step back to examine our work.

"Not bad for a first-timer," Percy jokes, her voice filled with amusement. "Can we take a selfie?"

We stand with our backs to the tree as I snap a few pictures of us.

"It's getting late. I should start heading home," she says reluctantly.

Percy's packed me another meal to bring home. I put it in my messenger bag, and she walks me to the door.

"Thank you for tonight. I had a wonderful time," Percy says, her eyes shining with warmth.

"So did I." I feel a rush of affection as she stands on her tiptoes and places a gentle kiss on my lips. "I wish you didn't have to leave," she murmurs.

"I wish I didn't either," I admit, reluctant to part ways.

"Will you come over again tomorrow?"

"Aren't you going to get sick of cooking for me every night?" I tease, though secretly thrilled by the invitation.

"No. I like having someone to cook for."

"In that case, it's a date," I say with a smile, already looking forward to tomorrow.

After another kiss goodnight, I start the walk home. My apartment's about two miles from Percy's. I'm thankful for having grown up in the city and being used to walking. It makes the twenty-minute walk home not too terrible. However, if this is going to be a long-term relationship, which I hope it will be, I might want to look into purchasing a car. It'd be quicker to get back and forth, and it would give me the ability to take Percy out more. She hasn't seen much, if anything, outside of Washington, and I want to show it all to her. To share all her firsts. Percy's known far too much hurt in her life. I intend to be the man who changes that—who gives her the world.

I'm not ashamed to admit I've fallen fast and hard. I'm in love with Persephone Douglas.

Percy and I have been inseparable. I've been staying in her guest room rather than going home every night. We've fallen into a comfortable routine of meeting Aurora and Chris for breakfast, working all day, and then returning to her house for dinner. She's even managing to teach me a few things about cooking. Tonight, we're making butternut squash stuffed shells.

"Christmas is next week," Percy says.

"Indeed, it is." I continue to mix the chopped spinach into the ricotta cheese.

"Are your parents coming in?" Percy pours the cut-up butternut squash into the cheese mixture.

"They are."

"Where are they staying?"

"I was going to have them stay at my apartment." I've been staying in Percy's guest room since last week.

"I guess you'll be going home to stay with them?"

I set the spoon in the bowl and pull Percy to me.

"Do you want me to stay there?"

"No." She hesitates. "I just thought—"

"Percy, we're adults. What we decide to do with each other is up to us."

"But you haven't decorated your apartment."

"I don't think they'll care." I shrug.

"And you don't have anywhere to sit and eat."

"That I don't have."

"What would you think if we had them here for Christmas dinner?" She looks uncertain. "They're welcome to stay here too. If you'd like."

"Mom and Dad would prefer the privacy of staying at my place. But I know they'll love coming here for dinner." I kiss her soft lips. "You're amazing, Percy."

"I'm nervous they won't like me."

"They're going to love you. Just like I do."

"What?"

"I love you, Percy. I know it might sound crazy, but I feel like I've known you all my life, and I'm completely head over heels in love with you." She studies me curiously but silently, and my stomach turns. "I just screwed everything up, didn't I?"

"No," she whispers. "I love you too, Duke."

I lift her and spin around with her in my arms. Percy throws her head back, laughing. She's just made me the happiest man in the world.

Percy

WE GET TO THE café for breakfast. Duke goes to sit with Chris, and I go into the kitchen to find Aurora. I need to talk to her. Some girl talk.

"Morning, Perc," Aurora greets me.

"I want to talk to you about something." I glance around to ensure privacy from the other guys.

"This sounds serious. Is everything okay?"

"Last night, Duke told me he loves me."

"Wow," she responds, setting down the tray of muffins she's about to put in the oven. "How do you feel about that?"

"I told him I love him too."

"Oh, Percy, I'm so happy for you. And Duke. But mostly you. You've waited a long time for this."

"Do you think it's too soon?"

"The more important question is, do you think it's too soon?" Aurora asks, her voice carrying a tone of genuine concern.

"I know it sounds crazy, but no. It feels like I've waited for him my entire life."

"You two are adults. All that matters is what you both want." The timer on her second oven goes off, and Aurora pulls out a tray of mini muffins.

"What are they?" I inquire.

"I'm trying something new for the signing."

"Oh, that."

"Are you still pouting about the event?"

I shrug. "Sometimes it's better to keep things a mystery is all."

"She says she loves M. Loveless's books, yet she isn't at all interested in learning their identity. Seems a little fishy to me."

"What?" My voice cracks as I grab the plates for breakfast and hurry out of the kitchen with Aurora on my heels.

"It's no secret you write romance. Maybe you're M. Loveless, and you don't want any of us to know," Aurora suggests.

Duke looks at me, and I roll my eyes. "As if."

"Did Percy tell you we're having my parents at her house for Christmas?" Duke asks, changing the subject.

Thank you, I mouth silently, and he takes my hand under the table.

"No, she didn't," Aurora answers.

"I was getting there. You guys and Earl are still coming, right?" Duke inquires.

"With Duke's family coming, we don't want to impose," Aurora responds.

"Don't be silly," Duke insists. "You're Percy's family. You'd never be imposing."

"Then, of course, we'll be there," Aurora confirms. "What about Houston and Laura?"

"They're flying to Kansas to spend the holiday with Laura's family," I inform them.

While we eat breakfast, we talk about everything that still needs to be done before the M. Loveless event. Part of me thinks I should've taken Janelle up on her offer of a decorator. I'm starting to doubt if we'll be able to pull this off.

"I'd love to stay longer, but it's time to open the store."

"Thanks for breakfast," Duke says and follows me to the door. "We'll see you guys later."

With Christmas being next week, the store is busier than usual. Between taking care of customers and finishing the displays for the M. Loveless event, I don't get a second to stop and take a breath.

The home office has been conducting remote interviews. So far, they've found one person who's supposed to start after the holidays. I wish it was sooner, but I understand their logic of not wanting me to have to train a new associate during our busiest time of the year and with the M. Loveless party coming up.

It's quieted down enough that I have some time to finish the window display for our New Year's Eve event. Gold and black streamers frame the store window. Five small tables are set up. Displayed on four tables are M. Loveless' mega hit books. The fifth table has a *Coming Soon* sign with some New Year's props, including a mock champagne bottle and glass. *Sweet Recognition* will be placed on that table in time for the party. Lastly, the backdrop is a life-size picture of M. Loveless' new book and all the information regarding the big event.

I know I shouldn't be, but I'm shocked at the response. Part of me assumed because the event was here in Washington, there'd be little to no interest. I mean, who really wants to come to our little town? Apparently, a lot of people. So many that we've had to forward the calls to the home office because our phones were ringing off the hook because we couldn't answer all the calls ourselves.

"Looks great." Duke pops his head around the curtain.

"Yep."

"Having M. Loveless here isn't that bad, is it?" he asks, helping me down the step to get out of the window.

I shrug. "I just think if someone wants to remain anonymous, they should be allowed to."

"How do you know they want to?"

"I don't. I'm just saying, no one should have to live in the public eye if they don't want to."

"If only the world worked that way." He kisses my cheek. "Are you ready to go? We need to get back to the house. The car will be delivered within the hour."

"I just have to grab my bag. I'll be right back."

Duke purchased a car online the other day. He said he wants us to have the option to go wherever we want, whenever we want. He was surprised when I told him I didn't have a driver's license. I've always walked everywhere, so I never had the need to get one.

"Ready."

We walk hand-in-hand back to my house, discussing everything we still need to do before his parents get here Friday, Christmas Eve. Their plane is arriving later in the afternoon, but Duke says we don't have to worry about picking them up because they've hired a driver.

"We'll need to stop at your apartment to tszuj it up," I suggest.

"Tszuji it up?" Duke questions.

"Freshen it up."

"I guess so," he replies with a shrug.

I giggle. "You guess so?"

"I don't typically get company, so I really didn't think about it," he admits.

"Maybe we can stop by tomorrow after work and get that done?" I propose.

"I can drive you in my new car." He gestures ahead of us. "Which looks like it's arriving now."

"It's gorgeous," I comment as we approach the striking blue Chevy Bolt.□Over the past few days, Duke has told me all the benefits of having an electric car. The Bolt is both pretty and eco-conscious without being expensive and flashy—something that's important to him. Looking at the vehicle now parked in front of my house, I'm sure he accomplished all his goals.

Over the past few days, Duke's told me all the benefits of having an electric car. The Bolt is both pretty and eco-conscious without being expensive and flashy—something that's important to him. Looking at the vehicle now parked in front of my house, I'm certain he accomplished all his goals.

We meet the delivery person in time for Duke to sign his name on the papers. Then, he's handed two sets of keys.

"One for you," he says, handing me a set.

"For me? I don't drive," I point out.

"Not yet, but I'll teach you," he reassures me.

"This is too much." I try to hand them back to him, but he refuses.

"I bought this for us. Let me do this for you," he insists.

The pleading look in his hazel eyes is my undoing.

"Fine."

Duke

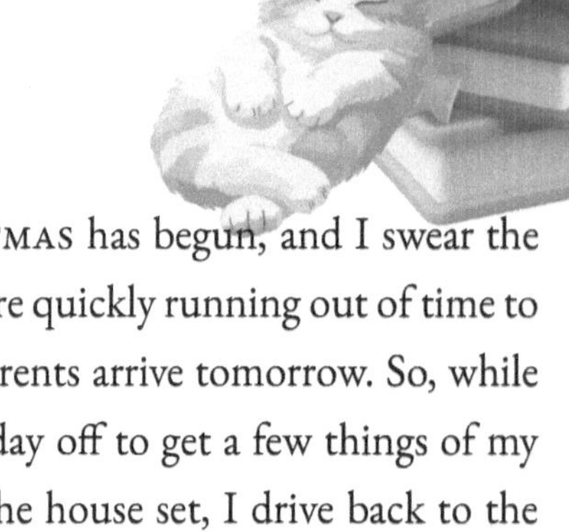

THE COUNTDOWN TO CHRISTMAS has begun, and I swear the clock is going at warp speed. We're quickly running out of time to prepare everything before my parents arrive tomorrow. So, while Percy worked today, I took the day off to get a few things of my own done. With everything at the house set, I drive back to the store to pick up Percy, who was able to get the afternoon off. The plan is to get as much done today as possible.

Duke:

I'm out front whenever you're ready.

Percy:

On my way.

A minute later, my beautiful girl is walking out of the store, and a smile lights up her face when she sees me.

"Hello, there, gorgeous." I lean over and kiss her when she gets into the car. "I missed you today."

"I missed you too." She buckles her belt.

"And we're off. First stop—my apartment," I say as I pull the car out of the parking lot and onto the road.

When we get to the house, I see the curtains in Mrs. Custis' front window shift to the side. The older woman doesn't miss a beat.

"Did you get a new car?" She pops her head out the door as we step onto the porch.

"I did."

"Hi, Mrs. Custis. How are you today?" Percy asks.

"No use complaining." She turns to me. "You haven't been home in a few days."

"No, ma'am. I haven't," I say as I unlock my door.

"When will your parents be here again?"

"Tomorrow."

"And you'll be staying here with them, I presume?"

"I'll still be staying at Percy's house."

Mrs. Custis looks back and forth between us disapprovingly. "Mhm. I see."

"We have a lot to get done," Percy says, taking my hand. "It was very nice seeing you."

Once we're inside the safety of my apartment, I turn to Percy. "I guess she doesn't approve of my sleepover."

"She's just a little old-fashioned."

My Percy is as beautiful inside as outside. She never has a mean word to say about anyone. She only sees the good in everyone and everything around her. I'm a lucky man.

"Okay, so what do we need to get done in here?" I ask.

Percy opens the fridge. "It's empty."

"No, it isn't. There's milk."

She picks up the half gallon. "It expired two weeks ago."

"Oops."

"We'll need to get some food and drinks."

"For?" I inquire.

"Your parents. I'm sure they'll appreciate having some of their favorites here in case they get snacky."

"That's a good idea."

"No," she says firmly.

Then, she looks at the empty spot in front of the window. "What about a tree?"

"A tree?" I echo, surprised.

"You know, a Christmas tree." She puts her hands on her hips.

"My parents aren't going to care if there's a tree. I promise."

"Fine," she concedes with a loud sigh. "Let's get the bed made. Then, we'll make sure there are clean towels and toiletries for them."

"Toiletries?" I repeat.

"Shampoos. Soaps. Toothbrushes."

"I'll put that stuff on the list, too."

I lead Percy down the narrow hall to my bedroom. She's never been in here, and I can't help the rapid pace of my heart as I turn the knob and push the door open.

"After you." I step aside.

She gives me an uncertain look before taking a tentative step into the room.

It's nothing fancy, not anything like her home. Like the rest of the apartment, the walls are off-white, and the floor is covered in an outdated mauve carpet. A full-size bed is against the interior wall, facing the small window that overlooks the street. To the right is a dresser, and to the left is a sliding door that opens to a tiny closet. Since I left most of my furniture in New York, having the apartment furnished, even if those furnishings are outdated, was a perk for me.

"Do you have an extra set of sheets?"

"That I do have." I open the closet, reach up to the shelf, and take down a set of white sheets.

Percy doesn't waste a second stripping the linens. Together, we put the fresh sheets on and remake the bed.

"Do you want to vacuum or wipe down the bathroom?" she asks.

"I'll do the bathroom." It's not her responsibility to clean my house, not that it's dirty. We're just tzjujing it up, as Percy says. Between the two of us, we're done in less than an hour. The house looks pristine.

With each minute that ticks by, I get more and more nervous. By the time we get back to Percy's house, I have to keep my hands in my pockets to hide the fact that they're shaking.

"I'm going to go up and change before I start dinner," Percy announces.

"Sounds good," I reply, nodding.□

I give her a few minutes head start, listening keenly for the sound of her bedroom door opening. Then, I bound up the steps two at a time to catch up.

Percy

I CAN'T WAIT TO get some comfortable clothes on and settle in for a cozy evening with Duke. When I get to my bedroom door, I find an envelope taped to it. For a brief second, panic courses through me. The last time I found an envelope—. This is not that, Percy, I silently remind myself.

The outside reads, *Little Did He Know...*

Carefully, I tear the envelope open and read the note inside.

Persephone,

A year ago, this city boy was feeling restless. He was looking for a change. By some stroke of fate, he turned on his television, and Washington, Georgia, was featured on a makeover show. He fell so in love with the spirit of the small town that he packed his belongings and set off for his new life. Only he didn't know just how big of an adventure it was going to be.

But there was a problem. The city boy had never lived in a small town and was feeling very alone and out of place.

He decided to take the bus into town, where he met a crazy cat lady and tasted the best muffin he'd ever eaten. The crazy cat lady also happened to be the most outgoing person he'd ever met, and the two struck up an instant friendship. When he told her about his job, she suggested he check out the bookstore next door because they had free internet. The city boy suspects the crazy cat lady also had ulterior motives.

Little did he know his next step would change his life forever.

When he walked into the bookstore, he laid eyes on the most beautiful woman he'd ever seen. It's a day he'll never forget. It was Dr. Seuss Day, and she was dressed as Thing One right down to the striped tights. On the floor in front of her were at least twenty-five young children, all attentively listening to her read 'The Cat in the Hat.'

When she looked up and saw the man, who was frozen in place staring, she smiled. The city boy was captivated by the depths of her blue eyes. Everything around him seemed to fade away, and the only thing that mattered was how he could get to know that woman. The problem was this beautiful woman was very shy.

Luckily for him, the crazy cat lady happened to be best friends with the woman and introduced them. But still, the beautiful woman remained shy, and the city boy didn't want to push. For nearly nine months, he waited patiently. Why, you ask? Because each day he saw her, he fell more in love.

Then, one day, the city boy thought he had lost his chance. He was heartbroken. Until the crazy cat lady set him straight. It was then he decided no more waiting. He sent the beautiful woman on a scavenger hunt, at the end of which he asked her out.

And much to his surprise, she said yes.

(Open your bedroom doors before you finish reading.)

Obeying the instructions on the note, I turn the handle and push open the double doors. When I step inside, I gasp. Set up all around the room are LED candles that flicker, mimicking real flames. I flip the page and continue reading.

Little did he know, she'd fall in love with him, too.

Little did he know, he'd want to spend the rest of his life with her.

The question is, does she want that too?

I swipe at the tears that are now streaming down my cheeks. I have to go to Duke. Spinning around, I find him standing just outside the doorway, watching me intently.

"How did you do all this?"

"I had some free time on my hands," he says as he steps into my room. "Percy, I know we've only been dating for a few weeks, but it feels like our souls have been connected much longer than that. I don't need more time to know I'm in love with you and want to spend the rest of my life by your side. The question is." Duke gets down on one knee. "Do you want to spend the rest of your life with me? Will you marry me?"

My hands cover my mouth as I try to compose myself enough to answer him. "I very much want to spend the rest of my life with you. Yes, I'll marry you."

Duke rises from his kneeling position and reaches into his pocket, pulling out an engagement ring, which he slides onto my finger. It's not a traditional diamond. Instead, the main stone is a stunning sapphire with a diamond on each side. The stones are set on a band of embedded diamonds. "I hope you like it. I wanted to get something as unique and special as you. But if you don't like it, we can—"

"I love it."

Duke places his hands on my hips and pulls me to him, kissing me passionately.

I know this is the time. Over the past few weeks, we've talked about this—our first time. We agreed not to rush it or plan a specific time, trusting we'd know when it was right. When we'd give ourselves to each other.

Tonight is that night.

Percy

Last night was everything I'd imagined it would be and so much more. Duke was gentle as he made love to me. Another first we shared together. Then, I fell asleep in his arms. It was magical.

But this morning, it's back to real life.

I hate that I have to work on Christmas Eve, but we're only open for a half day. So, while he finishes his shower, I make pancakes. Duke's always surprised to see so many *regular* foods, as he calls them, that I can make as vegan dishes. While I cook, I can't help but stare at my engagement ring. It's a reminder that last night really did happen. I'm going to marry the man of my dreams.

"Something smells delicious in here," Duke says as he comes up behind me.

"I hope you like pancakes." I rest my head on his chest, and he kisses my neck.

"I love them."

While I finish cooking, Duke sets the table and pours our orange juice. When the pancakes are done, I put them on a serving dish and bring them to the table. We both make our plates and start to eat.

But the vibe in the room suddenly feels off. Duke isn't making eye contact, and he's gone completely silent.

"Are you okay?" Percy inquires, concern creasing her brow.

"Me? Yeah." He puts his fork down. "Not really. There's something we need to talk about."

"This sounds serious."

"It is." His phone rings. "It's just my parents. I'll call them later." He sends the call to voicemail.

"You're scaring me."

"It's about my job." His phone rings again.

"Maybe you should answer it."

He slides his finger across the screen. "Hello?" He puts the phone on speaker.

"I'm so glad you finally answered." Duke's mom sounds frazzled.

"Is everything alright?" he asks concerned.

"There's been a bit of an accident," she responds.

"What do you mean?" He sits up straighter.

"Dad and I were skiing last night and—"

"Since when do you and Dad ski?" Duke interrupts, his curiosity evident.

"We've been trying to do some new things. Anyway, your father fell."

"Did he get hurt?"

"He fractured his ankle. It's nothing serious. We didn't want you to be surprised when he arrived with a boot on his leg."

"Are you sure the trip isn't going to be too much on him? We can reschedule."

"Absolutely not. We wouldn't miss spending the holiday with you. And we can't wait to meet this Persephone you told us about."

"She's right here with me," Duke assures his mother over the phone.

"Hello, dear. We're so excited to meet you," his mother responds warmly.

"I am, too. I hope your husband is okay," Percy chimes in, her concern evident.

"Mak will be just fine. The doctor gave him some good pain meds for the flight," his mother reassures.

"We can't wait to see you both," Percy says, her anticipation palpable.

Duke continues chatting with his mom for a few more minutes. By the time he's off the phone, it's past time for them to head into town. Even though Percy is okay to walk, Duke insists on driving her to work.

"What were you saying about your job?" Percy asks as they get ready to leave.

"There are some things we need to discuss—"

This time, it's Percy's phone that rings.

"You should get that," Duke prompts her.

I swipe the green button. "Hi, Ror. What's up?"

"Chris just called. He's at the grocery store, and the car won't start. Do you think Duke can run over and give him a hand?"

"Of course. I'm heading that way as soon as I drop Percy off," Duke affirms.

"You're a lifesaver," Percy expresses her gratitude.

"I'll see you in a few hours." Percy leans over the center console and kisses Duke. "I love you."

"I love you more."

Duke

Today's setting up to be a crazy day already. After dropping Percy off, I drive to the grocery store to help Chris jump his car. Luckily, it started right away, and then he was off to bring Aurora the supplies he bought for the author event next week.

Now, it's my turn to shop. I grab a cart and then pull the shopping list from my pocket. I need to do some last-minute things for our holiday dinner and some stuff for my apartment for my parents.

The grocery store is a madhouse. Seems I'm not the only last-minute shopper hoping to score everything on my list before the store closes in an hour. Fortunately for me, I'm able to get everything I need and get out with time to spare. I drop off the groceries at Percy's, then drive into town to pick her up.

"How long do we have until they get here?" Percy asks.

"Mom texted about an hour ago that they landed and are already on the highway. So, I guess we have a little over an hour." We gave my parents' driver directions to Percy's house. He'll drop them off and then go to my place to unload their things.

She bites her bottom lip.

"They're going to love you. Don't worry." I put my arms around her, wishing we had a little more time to be alone. "Are we all set here?"

"I think so."

"Let's get back to your place so we can get dinner started."

In addition to our vegan dishes, my fiancée is going over and above making a turkey breast for my parents. *My fiancée.* I love the way that sounds.

We're in the kitchen working on the finishing touches for dinner when the doorbell rings.

"They're here." We make our way to the door. "Mom. Dad. It's so nice to see you both."

Mom doesn't waste a second before pulling me into a hug. "Oh, Duke. We've missed you so much."

"I've missed you too."

Dad gives me a hug. "You look good, son."

"Come on in." I step aside to let them into the house. "Percy, I'd like to introduce you to my mom, Maggie, and my dad, Mak."

"It's so nice to meet you both." I can see her hands shaking.

"We've heard so much about the woman who stole our son's heart." Mom grabs Percy, pulling her in for a hug. "I'm glad to finally meet you."

"Did you have a good flight?"

"There was a little turbulence, but it happens." Dad shrugs.

"Why don't you come in. Dinner's almost ready."

"Your home is beautiful. You live here all by yourself?" Mom asks as she follows us into the kitchen.

"Me and my cats." Percy smiles. "Actually, it's the house I grew up in."

"We can give you the grand tour after we eat," I offer.

"That would be lovely."

I get my parents settled at the table with a glass of wine while Percy and I get the food on serving dishes.

"Is there anything I can help with?" Mom asks.

"We've got it."

It takes a few trips, but we manage to get everything onto the table. Then, we join my parents.

"There's enough here for an army. And it all looks delicious."

"Percy's an amazing cook." I take her hand under the table.

"Help yourselves, please."

Everyone fills their plates and begins eating. My parents can't stop gushing about Percy's excellent cooking.

"How's work?" Dad asks. "Have you been able to get enough jobs without living in the city?"

"Overall, yes. Most clients don't care where I live as long as I deliver a quality product."

"That's good to hear."

I don't really want to talk about work on a holiday, so I change the subject. "We have something very important to share."

"Oh?" Mom asks.

"Last night, I asked Percy to marry me, and she said yes."

"My baby boy is getting married," Mom exclaims and dabs at the corners of her eyes.

"That was a bit unexpected," Dad says.

"I know it may seem fast, but Percy's the other half of my heart. I can't imagine a future without her in it." I bring her hand, which is joined with mine, to my lips.

"As long as you're both sure, you have our full support." Dad picks up his wine glass. "To the happy couple."

We clink our glasses together in a toast.

Percy

DUKE SURPRISED ME BY telling his parents about our engagement in the middle of dinner. I wasn't half as surprised as they were, given the looks on their faces. Based on his dad's initial reaction, I was terrified they'd object to our engagement, but I was wrong. They were both very happy for us.

"Is that your ring?" Maggie motions to my left hand.

"It is." I extend my hand so she can see it.

"It's stunning. Have you set a date?"

"Not yet."

"I don't know about Percy, but I don't want a long engagement. I'd like to get married right away."

"A summer wedding in the city will be wonderful. If we start now, we'll have just enough time to plan something appropriate."

"The city?" I ask.

"New York City, of course."

I nearly choke on my bite of food. "Oh. I. Um."

"We haven't had a chance to discuss venues, but I think we'd prefer something small and private." Duke looks at me. "Here in Washington."

"I'd like that, yes," I say quietly.

I used to daydream about getting married. I think every girl has at some point. I'd wear a beautiful white dress, like a princess. Then, I'd thread my arm with my father's as he walked me down the aisle to give me away to the man I loved. Then my father was gone. After his death, I stopped dreaming about the future.

"We don't have to make any plans tonight," Mak says. "It's a holiday. Let's just enjoy one another's company." He gives me a knowing wink that I return with a smile.

After dinner, we move to the living room. Duke turns the fireplace on, less for heat and more for ambiance, and puts Christmas music on low before settling next to me on the couch.

"You did that skiing?" He points to his dad's foot. "Since when do you ski?"

"As your mom said, we've been trying out new activities to stay active."

"And you jumped right to skiing?"

Mak shrugs. "It was fun. Until this." He laughs.

After some ribbing, Mak asks Duke more about work. The two men discuss the websites Duke's been working on. I didn't realize he freelanced for some of the country's largest businesses. I'm in awe as I listen to him tell his dad about all his recent accomplishments.

"The best project lately has been for Muffins and Meows," he says matter-of-factly.

"What are Muffins and Meows?"

"It's a little café downtown. Percy's best friend owns it. It might not be for a big corporation, but I love the mission behind it."

"What do you do for a living?" Maggie asks.

I'm certain this is when things will fall apart. Both Duke and his parents are extremely accomplished. There's no way they're going to be okay with him marrying a girl like me.

"I work at a bookstore in town."

"She's actually the store manager."

"Did you go to school for business?" Mak asks.

"No, sir. I didn't attend college."

"Percy not only manages the bookstore, but she's also an author," Duke says proudly.

"What kind of books do you write, dear?"

"I don't exactly write books. I write romance stories on an online platform," I say, wishing I could curl into a ball and disappear. "It's really nothing. Working at the store is my actual job."

"She's being modest. I've read some of her stuff. She's quite good."

"Duke tells me you were a pediatrician." I desperately attempt to change the subject. "That must have been a very rewarding job."

"Overall, yes. I enjoyed my work very much. Of course, there were some difficult moments as well. But I wouldn't have done anything any different."

The more we talk, the more his parents seem to let their guard down. By the time we're saying goodbye for the evening, I decidedly like Maggie and Mak and feel very comfortable with them.

"Mrs. Custis knows to expect you," Duke explains. "The kitchen is totally stocked. If you need anything, give me a call, and I'll come right over."

"I think we'll manage just fine." Mak clasps his son's shoulder.

"Thank you again for inviting us," Maggie says and hugs me.

"I'm so glad you were both able to make it."

"We'll see you two tomorrow afternoon," Mak says, taking his wife's hand and walking down the path to their waiting driver and car.

Duke

I KNEW MY PARENTS were going to adore Percy. I mean, what's not to love? They can come off a bit prickly at first, but that's only the exterior they've learned to wear from all their years in the city. Once they get comfortable and drop their outer shell, they're totally different people. That's when Percy and my folks were really able to connect with each other.

"Are you ready for bed?" Percy asks.

"I am," I reply.

Percy squeals when I scoop her up and cradle her against my chest.

"You're going to hurt yourself," she warns.

"Never."

I climb the steps with her in my arms and take her to bed.

I wake the following day with Percy's arm thrown over my chest. Gently, I run my fingers through her pink hair. I don't know what

I did to deserve this woman in my arms, but I'll work every day to ensure I'm worthy of her love.

"Merry Christmas," she says quietly, her voice still groggy from sleep.

"Merry Christmas, sweetheart."

After spending a lazy morning in bed, we make our way downstairs. While I make coffee, Percy feeds our demanding feline trio. Then, I surprise Percy with breakfast. It's nothing fancy, just a bowl of oatmeal and fresh fruit. Despite the simplicity of the meal, she makes me feel like a million dollars.

"Are you ready to get to the presents?" she asks, her eyes twinkling with excitement.

"I am."

We agreed on two presents each.

"Can I go first?" She passes me the first gift.

I tear the paper from the neatly wrapped box. Opening it, I find a brand-new messenger bag with my name embroidered on the front.

"My old one was falling apart. I love this."

She passes me the second gift. Under the paper, I find a small, white box that gives no hint as to what's inside. I'm genuinely speechless, looking at its contents.

"Does this mean what I think it means?"

She nods. "I thought maybe you might want to officially move in. You don't have to—"

"I'd love nothing more. This is perfect." Now, it's my turn. I reach under the tree to get the two gifts I have for Percy.

She opens the first one. It's a signed copy of one of her favorite romance books, *Tears of Tess.* The author lives in New Zealand and only offers a minimal number of hand-signed copies.

"Oh my gosh, Duke. This is incredible," she exclaims.

"Open the next one." This is the gift I've been dying to tell her about. I bought it before I proposed, hoping she didn't say no.

She rips the paper off and, like my gift, finds a nondescript box. She looks at me and raises an eyebrow.

"Go ahead," I encourage her to open the box.

She lifts the lid and finds a folded paper inside. She opens it and begins reading silently. When she realizes what it is, she gasps. Inside the box are two plane tickets and hotel accommodations for us in Key West, Florida. "Duke, this is way too much."

"I know we haven't discussed a wedding date, but I was serious when I said I wanted to marry you as fast as possible. Then, I want to take you to Key West for a honeymoon. While we're there, we'll spend a day at Ernest Hemingway's house."

She's yet to speak. Her hands cover her mouth while tears trickle down her cheeks.

"You don't like it?"

She shakes her head. "I more than like it." She launches herself at me, peppering my face with kisses. "I love it."

The doorbell rings, and I drop my head back.

"I have no idea who that could be." She climbs off my lap and walks to the foyer. "It's your parents. I didn't think they were coming until later. We're not even dressed."

I groan as I stand from the couch and follow her to the front door.

"You guys are early." "Your mom insisted." Dad rolls his eyes. "I told her we should wait."

"Come on in."

We make coffee and get them settled in while we go upstairs and get dressed. When we come back down, we exchange gifts with my parents, and then, since the weather is beautiful, we take advantage and go outside on the patio. I get the fire lit, and we sit while my parents tell stories about me as a child.

A short while later, Aurora, Chris, and Earl arrive. Mom goes into the house with the girls to get dinner ready while the three of us guys stay outside and talk.

Never would I have guessed my life in this tiny town could be so full.

Percy

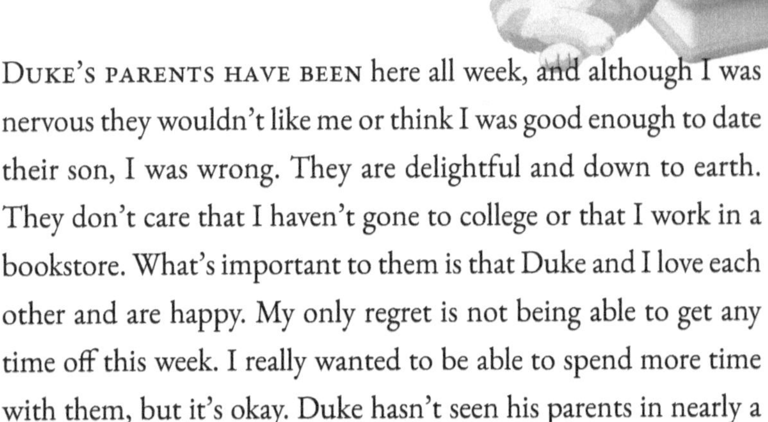

Duke's parents have been here all week, and although I was nervous they wouldn't like me or think I was good enough to date their son, I was wrong. They are delightful and down to earth. They don't care that I haven't gone to college or that I work in a bookstore. What's important to them is that Duke and I love each other and are happy. My only regret is not being able to get any time off this week. I really wanted to be able to spend more time with them, but it's okay. Duke hasn't seen his parents in nearly a year, so I'm glad they're getting this time to catch up.

Last night, we were all at the store until late. Turns out Maggie is very talented when it comes to decorating. I was more than happy to turn the reigns over to her. The final product is exquisite. Nooks with Books is officially ready for an upscale New Year's Eve party.

And it's a good thing because tonight's the big night. Janelle flew into town last night and has been with us at the store since bright and early this morning. She's coordinating not only the flowers and food but also the rental company that's currently setting up tables and chairs outside the store for any overflow of attendees. I'm told we're expecting nearly two hundred and fifty people—something I didn't need to know. That knowledge has only made me more nervous about tonight.

"I love your friend's café," Janelle says as she walks into the store. "Everything's set over there. She'll be ready to go for eleven."

"The Hot Box staff is setting up their food display." I motion to the other side of the store. "Everything appears to be on schedule." Except for me. It's almost eight o'clock, and I've not been able to go home to get dressed.

"Madeleine texted and said everything's set on her end as well." Janelle takes a deep breath. "I can handle everything here. Why don't you go home and get yourself ready for the big event." She gives me a knowing smile.

"I'd appreciate that." I motion to Duke. "You ready to go?" He gets up from where he's been sitting, patiently waiting for the past hour. Duke takes my hand and leads me out to the car. I'll admit, when he brought up the idea of getting a car, I didn't see the value in it. But it's come in handy with all the trips back and forth.

"My parents are on their way to your house as we speak," Duke says. "They are bringing take-out."

"That sounds great. I'm starving."

We pull up at the same time as his parents. Duke hurries over to help his father carry the Chinese take-out bags into the house. Maggie doesn't waste a second telling me about their day. They're quickly falling in love with the slower pace of life Washington offers.

After we eat, Duke sends me upstairs to shower and start getting ready while he cleans up and does the dishes.

I'm sitting in my bathrobe, drying my hair, when Duke comes into the room. He stands behind me with a serious look as he watches my movements in the mirror.

I turn the blow dryer off. "Is everything okay?"

"It is."

"Are you sure?"

"I'm just nervous knowing how many people are going to be at the store tonight. Big crowds were never my thing."

"Tell me about it. I wish I could skip the whole thing."

"I'm going to go take a quick shower." He kisses the top of my head and then disappears into the ensuite.

I'm putting the last of the pins in my updo when Duke comes out of the bathroom wearing a towel.

"If this is supposed to make me want to go tonight, it's having the opposite reaction."

He laughs, a deep throaty sound that makes my insides quiver. "It's only a few hours, then it'll be over. Right?"

"Right," I say, far less certain than I'm feeling.

I've been putting off getting dressed, but I'm running out of time. I slip into a black swing dress with a sweetheart neckline that I've paired with red heels. My outfit for tonight is very out of character, but I wanted to be understated.

"Can you help me with the back?" Duke slowly drags the zipper up. "You look stunning." He kisses my neck.

"You don't look half bad yourself, Mr. Kennedy." Actually, he looks mouthwateringly delicious in his black suit.

"Ready?" he asks.

"As I'll ever be." We walk downstairs and find Duke's parents in the living room.

"Look at the two of you. You make a gorgeous couple." Maggie smiles, but as we get closer, her smile fades. "Duke, come here in the light."

"Why?"

She examines him closely. "This is the wrong jacket. It's blue, not black."

"Do you think anyone will notice?" I ask.

"I do," she says without hesitation.

He looks back and forth between his mom and me. "Why don't you go ahead with my parents, and I'll run back to the apartment. I'm assuming the black jacket is on the hanger with the blue pants." He shrugs. "I'll meet you there as soon as possible."

"Okay."

He kisses my cheek and rushes out the door.

The driver pulls to a stop in front of the store and then comes around to open the door. Everyone turns to look at us as we exit the car. For a moment, I feel like royalty. That is, until nerves set in. There's already a long line outside the door. Duke's father is a perfect gentleman and guides Maggie and me past the crowd and into the safety of the store.

"Persephone, you look exquisite." Janelle hurries over.

"Thank you." I smile nervously. "I'd like you to meet Maggie and Mak Kennedy, Duke's parents."

"It's a pleasure to meet you both." Janelle looks over my shoulder. "Where's Duke?"

"He had to run back to his apartment to change his jacket. He'll be along shortly."

We busy ourselves with the final details before the event. The minutes tick by, and there's still no sign of Duke. I'm beginning to get worried, so I finally give in and text him.

Percy:

> **Where are you?**

It takes a minute for the message to show as read. Then, the chat bubbles dance on the screen.

Duke:

> Mrs. Custis had an emergency. She needed my help.

Percy:

> **Is she okay?**

Duke:

> Yes. A fuse blew. It's not my forte, so it took me a bit to figure it out. I'll be there as soon as I can.

Percy:

> **Drive safe.**

I'm updating Duke's parents on his arrival when Janelle comes over.

"Madeleine and M. Loveless are on their way," she squeals.

"I'll open the doors." As soon as I do, women and a few men begin pouring into the store. The excitement is contagious, and despite my misgivings, a small part of me can't help my curiosity.

"I guess you aren't M. Loveless," Houston says.

"Sorry to disappoint you."

"It's okay. All will be revealed in a few minutes."

"It will."

The crowd's energy is explosive when a limousine with dark-tinted windows pulls up in front of the store. A driver steps around the front of the car and opens the back door. A beautiful woman with chestnut brown hair gracefully steps out of the limo. As soon as she's out of the vehicle, the driver quickly closes the door.

"Do you think that's M. Loveless?" Houston whispers.

"No. That's the publicity executive from His One, Her Only Publishing," Janelle says as she walks past us. "Good evening, Madeleine."

"It's so nice to finally meet in person." The two women shake hands.

"I'd like to introduce you to Persephone and Houston."

"It's lovely to meet you both."

"You as well."

"The store looks incredible." Madeleine looks around and smiles. "Are we ready for the big reveal?"

Janelle looks at me, and I nod. "I think we are," she says.

Madeleine gestures to the crowd, quieting them. "Thank you for joining us on this New Year's Eve. I know you're all very excited to learn the identity of your favorite romance author, M. Loveless."

The crowd claps and cheers. Cell phones are held up all around the store, catching this moment on camera.

"I don't want to keep you waiting any longer." She gives the driver a small wave. He nods in response and turns to open the door.

My eyes are glued to the figure stepping out of the limousine.

"Duke?" My voice is barely a whisper.

Duke

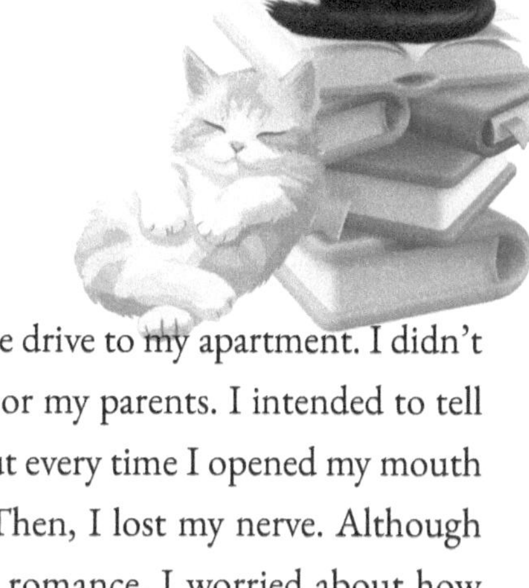

Guilt eats away at me on the drive to my apartment. I didn't intend on having to lie to Percy or my parents. I intended to tell her before my parents arrived, but every time I opened my mouth to speak, we were interrupted. Then, I lost my nerve. Although Percy loves reading and writing romance, I worried about how she'd feel about a man being a romance author. Not just any man, the man she's engaged to. Once my parents got here, the holiday was officially underway, and things just went too fast.

Since I chickened out of telling Percy before tonight, I had to come up with a plan B. That's how this ridiculous idea of grabbing the wrong jacket was born. I knew my mom would spot the small detail, and I'd have an excuse to leave.

Percy's initially going to be shocked, that I'm certain of. But I'm sure that once she gets past it, she'll get a good laugh at all this. As for my parents, I'm not sure how they're going to feel learning their son is a romance author. After the event, Percy and I can talk. If she doesn't want to marry a romance author, I'm more than okay with walking away from writing—it was never in the plan for my future, anyway.

I have just enough time to change my jacket before I get a text.

Madeleine:

I'm outside.

I take a quick look out my bedroom window. Sure enough, there's a black limousine sitting outside. This is really happening.

Duke:

I'll be out in a minute.

My phone dings again. This time, it isn't Madeleine.

Percy:

Where are you?

She must be going crazy wondering where I am.

Duke:

Mrs. Custis had an emergency. She needed my help.

Percy:

Is she okay?

Duke:

Yes. A fuse blew. It's not my forte, so it took me a bit to figure it out. I'll be there as soon as I can.

Percy:

Drive safe.

I slide my phone into my pocket and walk out to the limo. The driver is waiting outside the door. When he sees me, he opens the door.

"Thank you," I say as I get into the car.

"Mr. Loveless?" Madeleine asks, confusion written all over her face.

"Please, call me Duke. You must be Madeleine."

"I am." She schools her features. "I'm sorry, I was expecting—"

"A woman?"

"Yes." She smiles. "Wow. The readers are going to be shocked."

On the short drive into town, Madeleine fills me in on all the details of tonight's signing. But I'm only half listening. The other part of me is worrying that this wasn't a good idea. That I should've stuck to my initial stance of remaining anonymous. The problem is, it's too late to change my mind now. The driver slows to a stop in front of Nooks with Books, which is crawling with people.

"Wait here until I'm sure they're ready," Madeleine says. "The driver will open the door when it's your turn."

"Okay." I remain glued to the buttery, soft leather seat, knowing that once I step out of this vehicle, my life and the lives of everyone I care about will be irrevocably changed.

Just as Madeleine promised, the driver opens the door a second time. "They're ready for you, Mr. Loveless."

"Thank you," I say and step onto the sidewalk.

Part of me registers the screams and applause from the crowd gathered, but the only thing that matters is the woman standing just inside the bookstore. She's not smiling. There's not a trace of humor or excitement on her face. Instead, tears pool in her blue eyes.

Madeleine walks to where I stand, frozen in the doorway. She gives the crowd a moment to settle down. My heart hurts knowing I've caused Percy pain, and I'm helpless to stop it.

When the store becomes quiet, Madeleine speaks. "Ladies and gentlemen, I'm pleased to introduce you to M. Loveless." The volume in the store rises to an unbelievable roar.

Aurora pushes her way through the crowd to be at Percy's side. She wraps her arm around her friend, trying to console her.

"You've all been very patient, so let's get this signing underway," Madeleine announces as she leads me to a table that's been set up at the back of the store.

"Can I just have a minute?"

"I'm afraid not. It's going to take hours to get through all these people. Whatever it is will have to wait."

I follow her to the back of the store, where Houston and Janelle are already waiting by the signing table. "I don't know what to say." Houston shakes his head in disbelief. "You should've at least told Percy."

"I tried." My heart breaks as I watch Aurora trying to console a now sobbing Percy. We're interrupted by a reader placing a book in front of me. Mindlessly, I sign my name. "Would you please check on her? Tell her I need to talk to her."

"Can I get a selfie?" The woman in front of me asks.

"Sure." I put on a fake smile for the picture and then turn my attention back to Houston. "Please. If not for me, for Percy."

"I'll talk to her," he says and walks away.

While I continue to sign books and smile for pictures, I try to keep an eye on Percy. Eventually, my parents make their way to her. Mom glances back at me, a similar look of shock on her face, before she reaches out to hug Percy. My arms should be the ones consoling her, but instead, I'm stuck at this table. When Percy finishes talking to my parents, Chris puts his arm around Percy and escorts her out the front door. Houston returns to the table a few minutes later.

"Where did she go?" I ask, scanning the room.

"She went home," he replies, his voice tinged with sadness.

I'm able to take a few minutes to speak with my parents while we pause to ring in the New Year.

"Is Percy okay?"

"No," Dad says flatly. "She's not okay at all."

"This wasn't how it all was supposed to happen."

"I don't think I understand," Mom says. "You write romance books?"

"Yes."

"I thought you built websites."

"I do that too. It's a long story, and I'd like to explain it to you." I look back at the table where Madeleine's waving for me to return. "I just can't right now."

"This is a lot for us, too." Dad puts his arm around Mom. "We're going back to your apartment to try to wrap our heads around this."

By the time I sign the last of the books and the store clears out, it's after two a.m. I'm exhausted and worried about Percy. I've tried texting her a few times, but she's not returning any of them. Heck, she's not even reading them. I drop my head into my hands.

"I can't believe you're M. Loveless," Aurora says and sits in the chair next to me.

"Surprise," I say wryly. "I'm afraid I ruined everything with Percy."

"She was shocked. But she'll get over it."

I wish I could believe her. After seeing the look on Percy's face when I walked in, I'm not sure that's the truth. "What do I do?"

"Talk to her. Explain it all."

"That's exactly what I tried to do. But every time I went to tell her, we got interrupted. Then, I talked myself into thinking she'd find it funny. I never meant to hurt her."

"I know that. Once Percy has the chance to get over the shock, she'll see that too," Aurora reassures me. "I have to ask, though. How did you end up writing romance novels?"

"It's a very long story. Can I tell you another day? I really need to go to Percy."

"Of course. Just be gentle with her."

I'm making my way to the front of the store when Madeleine steps out of an aisle. "Duke, we'd like to do some publicity photos to use—"

"I can't. I have somewhere I need to be."

"The photographer is here." Madeleine hurries to catch up. "You can't just walk out."

My legs are longer, and my pace is faster. I close the door behind me and hurry down the street to where I see the limo parked.

Percy

I STAND OFF TO the side and watch as Duke—my Duke, is escorted to the back of the store by Madeleine.

Duke is M. Loveless.

I'm engaged to this man who didn't consider telling me the truth. Instead, he allowed this bombshell to blindside me. He let me find out with all the other readers, none of whom have a personal interest in the man behind the books. If he kept this from me, what else is he not telling me? I don't want to cry in front of all these people, but I can't help it. I feel cold and numb as tears wet my face. Thankfully, Aurora appears at my side.

"You didn't know," she says, her voice filled with empathy.

I shake my head, feeling a mix of disbelief and betrayal.

"I can't believe your fiancé is M. Loveless. You have to admit, it's pretty cool," she remarks, trying to find a silver lining.

But there's no coolness in this revelation. He smiles as he signs books and takes selfies with fans, but that's not the man I know. The man I fell in love with. "I don't know who that man is," I murmur, my voice heavy with uncertainty.

"Give yourself a little time to process this," Aurora suggests, offering me a comforting squeeze. "He's still the same Duke."

"Percy honey, are you okay?" Maggie's concerned voice interrupts our conversation.

"I don't think so. Did you know about this?" I ask, my gaze searching for answers.

She glances back at her son. "We had no idea. We're just as shocked as you." With genuine concern, she wraps me in a hug. "I'm sure he has a very good explanation for this."

"Yeah. I'm sure he does," I mumble, though doubts gnaw at my mind.

"Duke sent me over to check on you," Houston says, appearing at my side. "Are you okay?"

"No." The walls of the store feel like they're closing in on me. "I need to get out of here."

"I'll take you home," Chris offers, stepping forward.

"Aurora needs you here," I protest weakly.

"I'll give her a hand until Chris gets back," Houston offers, understanding the urgency.

"Come on." Chris puts his arm around me, offering comfort, and leads me out of the bookstore.

Chris offered to stay until I calmed down, but I told him I was fine. I really needed to be alone. I haven't even bothered to turn the lights on. After I kick my shoes off, I grab a blanket and curl up with Tess in my dad's worn armchair, desperately trying to make sense of everything that occurred tonight. But I'm unsuccessful. No matter how hard I try or what spin I try to put on it, nothing about this makes any sense.

Why didn't he tell me the truth? Shouldn't he have done that before he proposed? Before he made love to me? My head throbs from crying.

I don't even know what time it is when I hear the front door open and then close.

"Percy? Where are you?" Duke calls.

Why is he here? I don't want to see him. Hopefully, if I stay quiet, he'll think I'm not here, and he'll leave. Much to my dismay, Tess jumps from my lap and rushes out to Duke, meowing loudly. Traitor. Duke steps into the library and turns the lights on.

"Why didn't you answer when I called for you?" Duke's voice is strained with emotion.

"I didn't want to," I admit, feeling the weight of her disappointment.

"Please give me a chance to explain." Duke approaches me, his expression pleading.

"There's nothing to explain. You lied to me," Percy accuses, her voice quivering with hurt.

Duke squats down to get at my eye level. "I tried—." His words trail off, his own anguish evident.

"If it was that important, you would've made sure I knew before you walked into the store tonight." Unwelcome tears fall once again. "I can't believe you did that to me."

"Every time I tried to tell you, we got interrupted. Before I knew it, it was tonight." He runs his hands through his hair. "I hoped you'd be surprised. I never thought you'd be mad."

I throw the blanket off my shoulders and stand, nearly knocking Duke over in the process. "You didn't think I'd be mad?" I yell. "We're supposed to be getting married. There shouldn't be any secrets between us."

Duke rises to his full height. "You're right. I shouldn't have walked in there until you knew. That's on me."

"I feel like I don't even know who you are," I express, my voice trembling with emotion.

"I'm still the same person. Nothing's changed," Duke insists, his tone pleading.

"Everything's changed," I counter, feeling the weight of the moment. With a trembling hand, I slide the engagement ring off my finger. Holding it out in my open palm, I offer it to him. "The wedding is off."

"Don't do this, Percy," Duke implores, his eyes reflecting a mix of sadness and desperation.

"You need to go back to your apartment. I'll get your stuff together and have it outside for you tomorrow," I assert, trying to remain firm despite the ache in my heart.

"I don't want us to be over," he pleads, reaching out to me.

I push the ring into his hand. "You need to leave."

If I don't get out of here, I will totally break down. I don't want to do that, so I push past him and run upstairs. It takes a few minutes until I hear the front door open and close.

In a matter of minutes, the dreams I allowed myself for the future Duke and I would share were shattered. I shouldn't have been stupid enough to allow myself to dream again.

I lie on my bed and cry myself to sleep.

Percy

I barely get any sleep. Instead, I toss and turn until I finally give up and get out of bed. After a cup of coffee and some acetaminophen, I grab a bag, collect Duke's things, and put them on the porch.

By mid-afternoon, I still haven't bothered to get dressed. The cats have been meowing and winding themselves around my feet. They want to go for our daily walk, but I don't plan on leaving the house. I'm taking a day to feel sorry for myself.

The doorbell rings, but I don't bother to get up to see who it is. A minute later, I get a text.

She doesn't reply, and I hope she's left, but that hope is squashed when I hear her walk into the house.

"Okay, maybe he should've told you before the party," Aurora concedes.

"Maybe?" I raise an eyebrow skeptically.

"I'm sure he has a good explanation for why he didn't," she tries to reassure me.

"It doesn't matter. We're over," I state firmly.

"Oh, Perc. Don't make any rash decisions," Aurora pleads.

"I already gave the ring back and called off the engagement," I remind her.

"I wish you'd reconsider," she sighs.

"Nope. Not a chance. If you're going to stay, I don't want to hear his name again," I declare.

"Whatever you say," she replies, though her giggle belies her acquiescence.

I'm glad Aurora thinks this situation is funny. If the shoe was on the other foot, I'm sure she'd see things a lot differently.

Duke

DEVASTATED. THAT WORD DOESN'T even come close to describing the emotions I'm experiencing as I walk away from Percy's house. She didn't give me a chance to explain everything to her. I understand her point that I shouldn't have let her find out like that, but at the moment, I didn't know what else to do. Between the holidays and my parents being here, time slipped away from me. Before I knew it, it was the night of the event, and I was sitting in a limousine outside the bookstore. I knew she'd be surprised, but I really thought it would be a good surprise. Not even for a second did I think it would break us up.

It's a lonely walk back to my apartment. When I arrive, I'm startled to find my father sitting on the sofa. "You're still up?" he asks.

"I couldn't sleep without getting some sort of an explanation," I reply.

I settle into the armchair across from him. "I really don't know where to start."

"How about the beginning?" he suggests.

"None of this was supposed to happen," I confess.

"Yet it did," he observes.

"Yes, sir," I nod.

"Help me understand," Dad requests as he leans back, crossing his arms over his chest.

I begin telling him about the wedding gift I gave Marcel and Kaida. "I wrote a story about how they met. I hired an artist to illustrate it with anime-type pictures based on their photos." What I didn't know was that Kaida had some friends in the publishing industry. She showed them the book I wrote, and they asked if I had any other works. "I'd been writing stories for a while. Stories where the underdog got the girl, you know?"

Dad nods but remains silent.

I was surprised that Kaida showed them what I wrote, and I was even more surprised that they liked it and wanted to read more. So, I sent them another manuscript I'd been working on, and they requested an in-person meeting. "I guess they really liked it because they offered me a contract and a sizeable advance."

"I see," Dad says.

"Personally, I thought the publisher was crazy. I told them I'd sign on the condition of anonymity. They had no problem with it. That's how M. Loveless was born." I shrug. "For some reason, my books resonate with readers, and they've kinda blown up."

"After we got home from the bookstore, I went online and read about your success." Dad shakes his head and chuckles. "I never imagined my son would be a bestselling romance author. Why didn't you tell us?"

"I didn't know how you and mom would react. I never planned to go public, and I figured what you didn't know didn't hurt anything."

"You're wrong there, son. Haven't we taught you from a young age the importance of honesty?"

"Of course."

"Then, you understand by withholding that information, you were being dishonest. We deserved the chance to know and to support you." He leans forward. "Persephone deserved the truth as well."

"I really screwed up, Dad," I confess.

"You did. Now, the question is, how are you going to fix it?" he asks.

"I went to her house to try to explain. But she gave me the ring back and called off the engagement," I explain.

"That's understandable. She feels betrayed," he acknowledges.

"But if she let me explain, I—" I start.

"You need to give her a little time and space to sort out her feelings," he interrupts.

"Then what?" I inquire.

"Then you have to live with the outcome," he says solemnly.

That's what I was afraid of. I don't want a future without Percy.

"You should get some sleep. Your mother has a million questions for you in the morning. I'm going to try to get some shut-eye. This was a very late night for an old man," he advises, clasping my shoulder as he walks by. "Hopefully, everything will work itself out."

Dad wasn't kidding. Mom woke me up just after sunrise and gave me a full inquisition. She, too, was disappointed I kept this from everyone. Although it will take her some time to wrap her head around this, she's supportive of my writing as long as it makes me happy. However, she did lay into me for keeping this from Percy.

While my parents pack for their flight home later tonight, I'm sitting on the couch, trying to figure out what my next step needs to be. How can I possibly get Percy to forgive me? My phone vibrates, and I rush to pick it up, hoping it's Percy.

Aurora:

> Percy asked me to text you. Your things are on the porch. She'd like you to leave the key inside the mailbox.

Duke:

> So, that's it? Can you tell her I really need to talk to her?

I wait for what feels like hours before I see Aurora's typing.

Aurora:

> She doesn't want to talk to you.

Duke:

> I don't want to lose her.

Aurora:

> She needs some time. Don't push, or she'll totally shut down.

Duke:

> Okay. I'll be by for my stuff in a bit.

Don't push. How do I not push when all I want to do is go over there and break the door down? To make her listen to me. To show her I'm the same person. Admittedly, I should've worked harder to tell her. To minimize the shock. But I didn't think she'd be upset. Foolishly, I thought she'd find it funny that her fiancé and one of her favorite romance authors are the same person.

I was so wrong.

Percy

Two weeks have gone by. Two long weeks without Duke. I've been going through the motions of life, but I'm numb on the inside. The pain is as great as it was when I saw Duke walk into the bookstore and be introduced as M. Loveless.

I might've been able to convince myself it was all a bad dream if it wasn't for the constant murmurings of the women in the bookstore. Every day they come in and carry on about M. Loveless being a gorgeous man and how they've heard he's single. It's a constant reminder that this is all very real.

And Duke? He hasn't been to the bookstore since. I know he's still in town because I see him sitting in the cafe every day. It doesn't bother me. There's no reason he and Aurora can't stay friends. I just won't go in there while he's there. It hurts too much.

Speaking of Aurora. She's still trying to convince me that this whole M. Loveless thing is no big deal. That Duke thought I might even find it funny. It doesn't bother me that he's a romance author or that he's M. Loveless. What bothers me the most, the thing I can't move past, is that he lied to me. Yes, lied by omission. But a lie is a lie. He was going to marry me, but he didn't trust me enough to tell me the truth. If he had told me, I wouldn't have felt the deep betrayal that washed over me when he stepped out of the limo.

He says he knows he should've tried harder to tell me. But since we don't have the ability to travel back in time, it doesn't make sense to talk about the what-ifs. I have to work on picking up the pieces and moving forward—alone.

The problem is that all my recent dreams and plans for my future involved Duke.

Now, I'm forced to make new plans—alone.

Duke

THE LAST THING I want to do is leave town right now, but here I am, packing my suitcase for a trip to New York City. It's a two-fold business trip. In addition to the websites I make, I've also been coding a security software program for one of my biggest tech clients. Now that the program is done, I have to install it on their main server. Then, I'm scheduled to do a presentation for their in-house tech team to teach them how to use it.

While I'm there, I'll also be stopping by His One, Her Only Publishing. The night of the signing, Madeleine wanted me to do a photo shoot, but I ran out on her. While I'm in the city, I've agreed to take some photos and an interview about my pen name and books. I'm not sure what's going to happen when my tech clients learn that I moonlight as a romance author. What little of the bottom is left may just fall out from under me.

I was hoping that by giving Percy some time and space that she'd come around, but she still isn't talking to me. With each day that passes, I'm more and more certain there's no coming back from the mess I made. And it's no one's fault other than my own. As much as I don't like it, I have to respect Percy's wishes and find a way to accept them. But I also don't want her to think I just skipped town. So, before I get on the highway to go to the airport, I stop by Muffins and Meows.

"Hey, Duke. How are you today?" Aurora asks sympathetically.

"Eh. No use complaining. It won't change anything," I reply with a shrug.

Aurora gives me a sad smile. "What can I get you?" she inquires, ready to take my order.

"I'll take a triple berry muffin to go," I request.

"Do you want a Lychee tea to go with it?" she offers.

"Sure, that'll be great," I agree as Aurora starts preparing my order. "I'm going to be out of town for a few weeks."

"Oh?" Aurora raises an eyebrow in curiosity.

"I have some business in New York City. I'm going to the airport when I leave here. My flight leaves tonight," I explain.

"I'm jealous. I'd love to see the city," Aurora remarks wistfully.

"You should go. It's unlike anywhere else in the world," I encourage her.

"Someday, maybe," she muses.

"I'm sure Chris will bring you," I suggest.

"About that. Chris is getting deployed in two weeks," Aurora reveals.

"Again?" I express surprise.

"Par for the course," she shrugs.

"Do you know where he's going?" I inquire.

"He can't say. We're planning on going to the courthouse next weekend to get married. It's not the wedding we dreamed about, but Chris really wants us to be legally married before he leaves," Aurora explains.

"I'm sorry things aren't working out the way you planned, but congratulations anyway," I offer my well wishes.

"I wish you were able to be there," Aurora expresses a hint of regret.

"Given everything that's happened, I think it's best if I'm not there," I admit.

"I haven't given up hope. You shouldn't either," Aurora encourages.

"I doubt she'll ask, but if she does, tell her I'm coming back," I request.

"I will. Have a safe trip," Aurora bids farewell.

With my muffin and tea in hand, I leave the café. Before I go back to my car, I peek in the bookstore window to get a glimpse of Percy. She's behind the counter waiting on a customer. Her usually vibrant pink hair is faded, and her face is pale with dark circles under her eyes. I'm concerned by what I see, but I'm helpless to do anything about it.

I've attempted to call her, but my calls go to voicemail, and my texts go unanswered. Chris suggested just going to the bookstore and making her talk to me. But that's where she works, not the place for airing our grievances. I could stand here all day and watch her, but if I don't leave now, I'm going to miss my flight.

With a reluctant sigh, I turn on my heels and walk away.

Percy

"He went back to New York City?" I ask, eyebrows furrowed with concern.

"Not for good, Aurora reassures me. "He said he'd be back in a few weeks."

Aurora turns around so I can zip up the short white dress she chose for her wedding today. She's trying to put up a brave front and keep a smile on her face, but I've known her a long time. I see past the façade to the sadness and fear she's desperately trying to hide.

The ceremony takes place inside a courtroom. It's short and informal, but the important thing is that Aurora and Chris leave the courthouse as husband and wife. I feel a pang of jealousy as Chris sweeps her off her feet and carries her to a waiting limousine.

I promised Aurora I'd go with her to the airbase to see Chris off. The scene around me is gut-wrenching. Couples, some with young children, tearfully embrace one another as they prepare for their loved ones to leave for another long deployment to an undisclosed location. I can't help but shed my own tears as I watch their emotional goodbyes.

With a final kiss, Chris slings his backpack over his shoulder and walks toward the military plane. Aurora turns and comes back to me. Her mascara is running down her cheeks, and she's trying to catch her breath. I put my arm around her, holding her tight, hoping to give her some strength to get through this.

"I'm scared, Perc," Aurora confides, her voice wavering.

"I know, Ror. Me too. But we have to be brave," I reassure her, wrapping an arm around her shoulder. "Chris is a well-trained soldier. He'll do what he needs to and come home to you safe and sound."

"He has to. He's going to be a daddy."

"You're pregnant?" I ask, surprised.

"I am."

"I'm so happy for you. Chris must be thrilled."

"I didn't tell him."

"Why not?"

"I don't want him distracted while he's doing whatever it is he'll be doing."

I understand her rationale, but it feels far too close to Duke not telling me about being an author. "That's a fine line."

"I know." The roar of the plane's engine drowns out our voices as it taxis down the runway and lifts off the ground. "I'll tell him. I'm just waiting for the right time."

◻

Percy

AURORA SPENT THE PAST two weeks at my house. She needed the company as much as I did. But last night, she went home. Aurora said she had felt sorry for herself long enough and that it was time for her to pick herself up and move forward. I wish I had her fortitude. I still haven't found my way.

Instead, I'm sitting on my couch, my cats snuggle around me while I flip through television channels. Since Houston has stepped into management and we've hired a few part-timers, my schedule has eased up. It's been so long since I've had a day off during the week that I don't know what's on TV. I stop flipping when I see Duke on the screen.

"Being a romance author is a female-lead profession. Were you nervous about revealing your identity as a male romance author?" The woman interviewing him asks.

"I was terrified, but not because of my gender. I already have a career. Still do. Writing romance novels, any novels, wasn't ever on my radar," he chuckles. "The reason I didn't want to go public is that I'm a very private person. I liked my quiet life, and I didn't want that to change."

The blonde smiles at him. "What's the reception been like since your identity has been revealed?"

"Readers have been overwhelmingly welcoming," I acknowledge.

"So, what's next for you?" she probes.

"As you can imagine, since New Year's Eve, things have been moving at hyper speed. For right now, I'm taking a step back to reevaluate things."

"Will we get to see another M. Loveless novel?" she presses.

"Possibly. We'll see what the future holds."

"Thank you so much for this very telling interview. M. Loveless' books are—"□

"Excuse me. I have one more thing I need to say," Duke interrupts the woman, and her fake smile falters. "There's an extraordinary woman who I hurt on New Year's Eve. Percy, I know I should've tried harder to make sure you knew who I was before the rest of the world found out. I have no excuse for that." He looks directly into the camera, and it feels like he's staring straight into my soul. "I screwed up, and I'm sorry. I love you. I'll always love you. I hope one day you can forgive me."

"Well, whoever Percy is," the reporter says, looking into the camera. "Hopefully, she heard that message."

I don't know what else the interviewer says. Her voice fades into the background. The camera zooms in on Duke, and I'm mesmerized by the pleading look in his eyes. He didn't have to say those things. Heck, he cut the interviewer off in order to get that message to me.

My phone starts ringing.

"Hello?"

"Oh my God. Duke was just on TV. You have to find the replay."

"I saw it."

"You did?" She shrieks so loud I have to hold the phone away from my ear. "You can't possibly stay mad at him after that."

"I have to go." I hang up the phone. I'm shaken and can't talk to anyone right now.

My mind drifts back to when I was an almost ten-year-old little girl whose mom had just walked out on her. Whose mom didn't say goodbye and never looked back. Never once sent a letter or called. I felt betrayed by the woman who supposedly loved me.

One night. That's how long I gave myself to cry. Then, instead of dealing with it in a healthy way, I constructed walls and put on a brave face. Never again would I allow someone to hurt me. The only two people I allowed behind those walls were my father and Aurora.

I was about sixteen when Dad sat me down.

"Persephone, what you're doing isn't healthy. You're punishing people for things they haven't done. You can't keep people at arm's length for the rest of your life."

"But Dad, if I let myself trust someone. Let them get close to me. They might hurt me."

"My sweet girl." He kissed the top of my head. *"Yes, you take the chance of getting hurt. Humans are not perfect. Even with our best efforts, we sometimes unintentionally hurt the ones we love the most. But you have to stop judging everyone through the lens of being betrayed in the past. Don't jump to conclusions. Love freely. And don't be afraid to forgive."*

I sat back and studied my father closely for the first time ever. Between the long hours at work and then coming home and being both mom and dad to me, I noticed he'd aged significantly in the years since mom left.

"If you could go back in time, would you still marry Mom? Even if you knew she'd eventually hurt you?"

"Yes," he said without hesitation. "Our marriage wasn't perfect. No marriage is. I'm not blameless in any of this."

"Don't say that. You made sure mom and I never wanted for anything. You were a good husband. It was mom that was the problem. She's the one who lef—"

"Persephone, you mustn't villainize your mother. I expected her to feel the same way I did about Washington. When she didn't, when she voiced her unhappiness, I turned a blind eye. I didn't consider her feelings or try to compromise." His eyes filled with tears. "But I loved your mom with all my heart. I still do. If she came home, I'd open my arms to her again, no questions. If it wasn't for our love, I wouldn't have you."

But then Dad left me, too, and I did exactly what he warned me not to do. Yes, I took a chance and let Duke get close to me. Then, I allowed all the hurts from my past, being abandoned by my mom and dad's death, to influence the way I reacted to him. He tried to explain, but I refused to hear him. At the first sign of trouble, I shut down and locked him out.

The night he proposed, he told me he had something important to tell me about his job. I assumed he meant his tech job. We got interrupted when his parents called. Once they got here, we were going nonstop, and we weren't able to get back to the conversation. If I'm honest, I didn't even think about it. But I went ahead and blamed Duke.

"I've been so wrong," I admit, desperately hoping it's not too late to mend what's broken.

Percy:

I'm sorry I hung up on you. I need your help with something.

Aurora:

Anything.

Percy:

I'll meet you for breakfast and fill you in.

Duke

My flight touched down in Atlanta late last night, then I had a nearly two-hour drive to Washington. By the time I get back to my apartment, I collapse in bed from exhaustion and sleep clear through the afternoon. When I wake up, I check my phone and find a text waiting for me.

Aurora:
Be at the café at six. Don't be late.

Duke:
I'm really not going to be good company tonight.

Aurora:
It'll be fine. Be there anyway.

Duke:
Why? What's going on?

Aurora:
Don't ask any questions. I won't answer them anyway. Just be here at six.

I debate ignoring Aurora's text and just rolling back over and sleeping away the rest of the day. The only reason I don't is because if I know Aurora, she'll end up beating on my door if I don't show up. In the end, I decide to go and see what she's up to.

Like every other Sunday, the small shops close early, and the downtown is deserted. It's exactly six o'clock when the bells jingle, announcing my arrival, but there's no sign of Aurora. I walk to the cat room and find her there sweeping the floor.

"I'm here," I say from the doorway, but she doesn't respond. Then, I notice she has headphones on. I walk over and tap her on the shoulder. "I'm here."

She pulls out the earbud. "I see that." She smiles brightly.

I search the room for my favorite redhead but don't see her. "Where's Pippi?"

"Duke, I'm sorry. She was adopted while you were away."

"Oh." I know I can't have a cat, but I've gotten very attached to Pippi and looked forward to seeing her every day. "Is there something you need?"

"As a matter of fact, yes. Come with me."

I follow her back into the main room of the café. She reaches under the counter and pulls out an envelope. "This is for you."

"What is it?"

"You'll have to open it to find out."

Duke

Uncertain of what I'll find inside the envelope, I step outside the café and tear it open. Inside is a piece of paper with a typed note.

To reach your destination, you will need to correctly follow these instructions:

After exiting Muffins and Meows, take a RIGHT to get on the RIGHT 'track,' which should bring you to the Georgia Woodlands Railroad station. If you're standing RIGHT in front of the historical marker, you can take a small leap and go RIGHT past the Washington Dance Academy. Continue RIGHT down the block to CJ's Pizzeria.

Don't be LEFT feeling thirsty, though. Step RIGHT into Padgett's Country Cafe and grab yourself a coffee so you will be LEFT with enough energy to finish this quest. Continue RIGHT past Washington Food Market, but don't be LEFT with a sugar craving. Step right into Kettle Creek Creamery to get a sweet treat.

Be sure to stop RIGHT in Hendricks and thank Michelle for the beautiful bouquet she made for me. Continuing on your journey, you'll want to pass RIGHT by The Pig and Bull Grill to find yourself on the brick path leading to the park. I'm sure once you pass by the kiddie playground, it will have LEFT you with fond memories of your childhood.

You should now be RIGHT next to the beautiful fountain in the middle of the park where, on warm summer nights in the past, have LEFT you in wonderment, gazing at the little lights strung all around the park. But don't be LEFT in your thoughts of the past. You still have a path RIGHT in front of you to traverse on the rest of this voyage.

You should find yourself RIGHT in front of the Austin Dabney bust, which would mean you're still on the RIGHT route. As you continue to the Mary Willis Library, stop and see if anyone LEFT any new, interesting books. Soon, you should find yourself RIGHT in front of the farmer's market and craft tents before making your way RIGHT out of the park and back onto Main Street.

Give a wave to Jon and Ashley at Summer House Realty so they won't be LEFT feeling ignored. As you travel two more blocks, you should pass Poss Ace Hardware- he always has the RIGHT tools for any repair job. You may be starting to wonder how much of this goose chase is LEFT? Well, you would be RIGHT to ponder this. So, why don't you stop when you get back to the café and turn LEFT, RIGHT into Nooks with Books to find what this odyssey was really all about.

 Percy

WITH THE LIGHTS OFF in the bookstore, I peek around the window's edge. Duke's standing outside reading the note. He picks his head up and looks up around as though he's expecting to find whoever wrote it to be standing there.

I start to worry when he doesn't move. What's he thinking? Will he follow the instructions, or will he crumble it up and go home? I'm ready to cheer when he turns right and starts the game. Now, the fun begins. Aurora and I walked the route twice to make sure we had the timing down. It should take Duke about an hour to complete his tasks. Which means I need to move fast.

Percy:

He just left.

"Wait here, Pippi. I'll be right back." The little red cat meows as I close the door to my office.

Even though I see him walk away, I'm still careful and only pop my head out the door just in case he's still on the street. Thankfully, I don't see him, so I hurry next door. Aurora's already pulling out the bag with the place settings and candles.

"You get started on this stuff. The food has a little bit to go. I'll bring it over as soon as it's done."

"I couldn't have pulled this off without your help."

"I know." She laughs. "Go, so you don't run out of time."

By the forty-five-minute mark, we've finished setting everything up. Aurora gives me a quick hug before she leaves.

Now, I wait.

It's another fifteen minutes before the door to the bookstore opens, and Duke walks in. The light from the LED candles reflects in his hazel eyes.

"Hi."

"Hi." He smiles.

"I see you found your way."

"I did." He steps closer to me. "Percy, please let me explain."

Duke

"WHY DON'T WE SIT down." She motions to a table that's set for two.

I pull out the chair for her and then sit across from her. She listens while I recount the story about the wedding gift and how I didn't know Kaida showed my writing to a publisher.

"Never in a million years did I imagine anyone would want to read something I wrote," I admit.

"Where did M. Loveless come from? Is it just a random pen name?" Percy inquires, her eyes wide with curiosity.

"No. But you have to promise you won't laugh."

"Cross my heart." She makes an X across her chest.

"Duke is short for Marmaduke." I chuckle at the absurdity of my name. "And Loveless is my mother's maiden name. M. Loveless."□

"Your name is Marmaduke?" Percy's eyebrows shoot up in surprise.

"My given name is Marmaduke Harold Kennedy Jr," I confirm.

"Wait a minute. Mak is also Marmaduke?"

I nod solemnly.

"Why didn't you tell me?"

"I've always despised my name. So, everyone only knows me as Duke."

"As if Persephone is a normal name?" She giggles.

"I love your name."

"Well, I love your name, Marmaduke."

"I should've tried harder. I should never have walked in here that night without telling you everything. I'm sorry."

"And I let past hurts get in the way. I shut you out, and I'm sorry."

"I love you, Persephone Douglas."

"If the whole M. Loveless thing is too weird say the word, and I'll walk away in a heartbeat. You're more important to me than writing books."

"I don't want you to walk away from writing. But I do need you to promise that no matter what it is, you'll never be afraid to tell me the truth," she says softly.

"I promise. I'll never keep anything from you again." I reach around my neck to unclasp the chain that holds her ring. Then, I get down on one knee. "Persephone, I'm still in love with you. My future is meaningless if you aren't by my side. Will you marry me?"

"Yes. A million times, yes."

I pull her to me and kiss her.

"Wait here." She pushes away. "I have a surprise for you, too."

She hurries down the hall to her office. When she comes back, she's holding a familiar red cat in her arms.

"I hope you don't mind a ready-made family?".

"Pippi?" I walk over to where Percy stands with Pippi. "Aurora told me she got adopted."

"She did." Percy grins. "By us."

I laugh out loud. This woman is always full of surprises. Life with her is going to be the most exciting adventure yet.

Percy

"I think I might throw up," I say to Aurora, who's buttoning up my wedding gown.

"If I made it through today without vomiting, you'll be fine." Aurora rubs her very round tummy.

She's due with baby number two, a boy, in a little over three weeks.

Although Duke and I wanted to get married right away, things didn't quite go as planned for us. After the New Year's Eve event, our lives changed dramatically. We decided to take our time adjusting to our new lives, which now includes a significant amount of travel back and forth to New York City. Another factor for us postponing our wedding was the life events our best friends were facing.

Shortly after the New Year's Eve event, construction was started to open the shared wall between Muffins and Meows and Nooks with Books. Now, customers can walk freely between the two businesses, which is great for everyone. That's the good news.

The not-so-good news is how much life for Chris and Aurora has changed over the past few years. Chris was injured on his last deployment. He was on a mission. We still don't know the location. All we know is he was clearing a town of IEDs when there was an explosion. It was a scary few weeks not knowing where he was and only being able to get spotty information. Finally, Aurora got word that he was safe at Walter Reed. Duke and I drove her to D.C. to be with him.

Chris was honorably discharged from the military due to his injury. It's been an adjustment for Chris to learn to use a prosthetic leg, but he's doing great. He's taken on the role of stay-at-home dad to their very busy two-year-old, Rayne, who's the flower girl in my wedding today.

When Aurora finishes my buttons, I turn around to face her.

"You look positively radiant." Aurora dabs at the tears in the corner of her eyes.

Not surprisingly, I've chosen a non-traditional gown for the ceremony today. It's a long, flowy strapless dress in a lavender ombre. My usual pink hair is currently my natural shade of blonde and hangs down my back in long, loose curls. I feel like a princess.

"He may not be here in person, but I know he's watching over you," Aurora reassures me.

There's a knock on my bedroom door.

"Who is it?" I inquire.

"It's me," a male voice calls out.

Aurora opens the door and lets Earl in.

"What do you think?" I ask the man who was my dad's best friend and who'll be walking me down the aisle.

Up until now, I've been able to keep my emotions in check, that is, until I see tears trickling down Earl's face. "You look beautiful, honey. Your father would be so proud." He wraps me in his warm embrace.

"Okay, enough crying. If we don't leave, Percy's going to be late for her own wedding." We share a laugh.

Then, the three of us walk downstairs to a waiting Chris and Rayne, who's asleep on her daddy's shoulder.

"You ladies look breathtaking," Chris remarks as he kisses his wife's cheek.

Duke wanted to make sure our wedding was fairy tale perfect. So, waiting for us outside the house are two carriages. One is white and is led by a black horse wearing a lavender bow. Chris, who's Duke's best man, and Aurora, who's obviously my matron of honor, are riding in it with Rayne.

The second is a carriage reminiscent of the one in the fairy tale *Cinderella* with two regal white horses. Earl and the driver offer me their hands to help me into the carriage as gracefully as possible. Once we're all seated, we start the ride downtown.

Our lives have been much different since Duke revealed his identity as M. Loveless. Washington is busier than usual, and for better or worse, our lives are more public than we'd always like.

But today, we chose to share our wedding with not only our friends and family but also with the romance book world. Our ceremony is being held under the gazebo in the Town Square. As we turn the corner, I see people gathered everywhere. Our carriage stops a block before the square while Chris and Aurora's carriage continues to the gazebo area. We wait while they climb out and get into place.

"Are you ready to marry your prince?" Earl asks with a smile.

"I think I've been ready my whole life."

"Let's go," he instructs the driver. Once again, our horses begin their clippity-clop cadence. Our stop is at the edge of the square, where we get out of the carriage. Janelle is waiting there to help straighten my dress before we begin our walk to meet Duke.

We get our cue, and "Here Comes the Sun" begins to play through speakers that are set up in the square. Earl puts his arm out for me to take.

"Don't forget this," Janelle says and hands me my bouquet.

A little over two years ago, our relationship started with a treasure hunt where I collected colorful paper flowers Duke made from the pages of books. Not just any books, M. Loveless's books. A clue I missed, by the way. Being sentimental, I saved the flowers. Today, they're my bouquet as I prepare to marry the man of my dreams.

From start to finish, our wedding is storybook-perfect.

The next morning, we left for our honeymoon. I was a bit nervous about taking my first plane trip, but my nerves disappeared once we were in the air. The view of the ground beneath us is unlike anything I've ever seen before.

For the past two weeks, we've been hidden away in a romantic oceanfront bungalow in Key West, Florida. But sadly, all good things must come to an end, and Duke's saved the best for last.

It's our final day in Florida, and we're going to Ernest Hemingway's house. We spend the entire afternoon exploring everything the island has to offer. Before we leave, we make a donation to help with the care of the polydactyl cats that call the island home.

Our marriage is still brand new, two weeks old, and I'm happier than I've ever been. Neither of us is perfect, but we're perfect for each other.

Shortly after our wedding, Percy left her job at Nooks with Books. We'd started a new venture that we weren't ready to share with the world yet, but one that was going to keep us both very busy. And it hasn't disappointed.

We've been traveling full-time since the day we left Key West.

You're wondering why?

~We're on a nationwide book signing tour for our new release, *Here Comes the Bride: The Underdog Finally Gets the Girl* by M. Loveless and P. Loveless.

Readers have welcomed us and our rom-com romance with open arms.

And for our story, the end is simple.

They lived happily ever after.

The End

Real Life Romance: Gilbert and Elizabeth https://geni.u s/GilbertandElizabeth

Also By Tara

Real Life Romance World

Real Life Romance: Gilbert and Elizabeth https://geni.u
s/GilbertandElizabeth

Real Life Romance: Duke and Percy https://geni.us/Duke
andPercy

About the Author

Tara Lynn is married to her soulmate, George. They are high school sweethearts who've just celebrated their 29th anniversary. Together they have four adult children, one son-in-love, and a grandson they're head over heals in love with.

Tara and George live in northeastern Pennsylvania but have the goal of one day living in an RV and traveling.

Tara hopes you fall in love with her sweet romance world, Real Life Romance. Each couple is meant to be one that might resemble a friend, family member, or even yourself. The stories will make you laugh and cry as each couple lives a real life and has a real romance. Although every couple and their story is unique, you can always count on a happily ever after.

Acknowledgements

FIRST AND FOREMOST, THANK you to my husband, **George**. I love being on this author adventure with you.

None of these books would be possible without your unending patience helping me to plot each book

and listen to draft after draft. That's not even getting to formatting and making the cover. You are

amazing and I wouldn't be able to do any of this without you. I love you.

To my kids: Thank you for being my biggest cheerleaders. Knowing I have your support means to world

to me. I love you all very much.

Mercedes G.- Thank you for the Date Idea. As soon as I saw it, I knew it was the one and who to go to for

help with it. Congratulations on winning the contest.

Amy: When I had the idea for a left/right, I knew you were the one to go to. Thank you so much for your

help. And congratulations getting your name on a book cover.

To the real-life Janelle: I'm so thankful I met you and for the friendship we share. And thank you for

giving me the idea to write a book about an author and booksellers. I hope you love the story.

To the real-life Madeleine: I'm so happy our paths have crossed and that we've become friends. I hope you like being the publisher in this story.

www.ingramcontent.com/pod-product-compliance
Lightning Source LLC
Chambersburg PA
CBHW030002010826
48973CB00007B/2133